The Fairies of
Nutfolk Wood

The Fairies of Nutfolk Wood

Barb Bentler Ullman

KATHERINE TEGEN BOOKS
An Imprint of HarperCollins*Publishers*

www.harperchildrens.com

Library of Congress Cataloging-in-Publication Data

Ullman, Barb Bentler.

The fairies of Nutfolk Wood / Barb Bentler Ullman.— 1st ed.

p.   cm.

Summary: After her parents divorce and she moves to the country with her
mother, fourth-grader Willa Jane, anxious and unhappy with the changes in her
life, discovers a world of little people called Nutfolk living in the woods around
her new home.

ISBN-10: 0-06-073614-3 (trade bdg.) — ISBN-13: 978-0-06-073614-9 (trade bdg.)
ISBN-10: 0-06-073615-1 (lib. bdg.) — ISBN-13: 978-0-06-073615-6 (lib. bdg.)

[1. Fairies—Fiction. 2. Friendship—Fiction. 3. Household, Moving—Fiction.
4. Divorce—Fiction.] I. Title.

PZ7.U335Fai 2006   2005028780

[Fic]—dc22   CIP

                                                                AC

Typography by Hilary Zarycky

1 2 3 4 5 6 7 8 9 10

❖

First Edition

For Sara and Riley

Contents

The Fairies of
Nutfolk Wood

CHAPTER 1

Stepping into the Tornado

"CHANGE IS LIKE A STORM," Mama said gently. "It's all windy and upsetting, but the sun has to come out eventually." She kissed my forehead and tried to smooth down my hair.

Grandma Cookie must have been eavesdropping from the dining room because she poked her head in and added sarcastically, "Maybe if '*Mrs. unfulfilled*' hadn't up and left her husband there wouldn't *be* any changes."

"Oh, Ma, for Pete's sake, give it a rest," Mama snapped. "I told you it was a *mutual* decision."

This led to some general bickering, which I tried to ignore as background noise, hearing it without listening.

I stared out the window of Grandma's front room and saw myself in the dusky glass. I didn't hardly recognize the girl in the window. She looked all scrawny and pinched, a little like Grandma Cookie.

Other kids had parents who'd gone through divorce. I don't know why I turned into such a basket case. I guess because if there is one thing I hate, it's change.

Change caused the storm in my dream that night. My worries and fears whipped into a cyclone, whirling around all of this *stuff*—the divorce, our house being sold, Daddy leaving, me feeling sick all the time. The dark funnel moved forward, creeping ever closer to Grandma's house.

I watched from her porch, petrified and filled with dread. When I tried to yell, all that came out was a whisper. Daddy appeared, and came running to save me, but the tornado grabbed him.

"Daddy!" I called. "Come back!" But just like that, he was gone.

Mama came out on the porch with her knitting. She said, "I've *had* it with this turmoil!" All of a sudden, the tornado sucked up her basket, and Mama jumped right in after it.

Grandma was in the living room screeching, "Hide in the basement!" I wanted to hide like anything, but I didn't want to stay with *Grandma*. I was afraid of the storm, but I couldn't stay put. Following Mama, I stepped into the tornado.

Up I went, twisting and swirling. I was afraid to go up and I was afraid to go down. My legs felt like rubber and my stomach flapped into my throat. I'd fling into something and be killed for sure. But I gained control, and found I could fly.

I swerved right out of that tornado and decided I'd fly to the mountains. I was convinced that if I could just get to the woods, everything would slow down. Everything would be safe and lovely, like all the picnics, and summer swims, and autumn walks at my uncle's mountain farm.

I flew to a spot in the woods where the ground seemed to shimmer and play tricks with the light. The plants were soft and close, the air smelled like warm pitch, and I wasn't scared anymore.

A small voice said, "Here is peace and courage, Willa Jane."

"Who's there?" I asked.

"Win some, lose some," the little voice said, giggling.

"Win some what?"

Ignoring my question, the child said, "We're country girls, you and I, no doubt."

The voice faded and was gone with the dream.

I woke in the hushed darkness of Grandma Cookie's spare bedroom. Mama slept in the other single bed, not three feet away.

"Mama," I whispered.

She answered immediately, "Waddya need, Wil?"

"I want to go to the country," I said.

"What country is that?"

"The country*side*. Like trees and mountains and fresh air. Like at Uncle Andrew's. Could we do that, Mama?"

"Sounds like a good plan, Sweet Pea."

We had been staying at Grandma Cookie's while the divorce went through and the house got sold. Daddy had left for California. He'd moved in with Uncle Jackson and Aunt Lena, and my *perfect* cousins, Rudy and Zack, who looked like models and had gobs of friends. Unlike me.

My best friend, Etta Myers, moved away last summer right before all the divorce talk. I wrote Etta long letters, but once she got settled, she wrote back less and less. Then I sort of lost interest in drumming up new friends. I knew I ought to try, but it seemed like so much work.

Daddy left after Christmas and it burned me up that he was leaving *me* to go stay with the perfect cousins. He wanted to go back to college, "to do something meaningful with his life." I guess that being my daddy wasn't meaningful enough.

Ever since then, Grandma Cookie made it her job to lecture Mama on the evils of divorce at every opportunity. "Blah-blah, you married too young. Blab-blab, the first divorce in the family. Yackety-yak, what kind of wife just gives up?"

Mama argued back, but it was pointless because Grandma Cookie had no intention of altering her opinion on anything, ever. I listened to it all, and it drove me crazy. My stomach was always churning and I forgot what normal felt like.

After missing a million days of school, Mama and my fourth-grade teacher, the principal, and the school psychologist all agreed to a home-school situation. What I needed was "security and consistency."

When we were alone, Mama said, "You don't have to think about school unless you *want* to think about school. Your studies can wait until you're back on your feet." She said it with conviction. But she looked around nervously, as if truant officers or school security could be skulking in Grandma's closets.

When Mama finally got her money out of the house settlement, she announced that we had overstayed our welcome at Grandma Cookie's. "It's time to get out of Dodge," she said.

"It's way past that time," I responded grimly.

She lowered her voice and confided, "It's all settled. We're going to Uncle Andrew's. I'll tell Grandma tonight."

The next day, in the dim light of early morning, we fled the city. With a twinkle in her eye, Mama noisily revved the Honda and squealed away from the curb, speeding down the block without a backward glance.

I looked back. Grandma Cookie watched from the porch and waved good-bye, looking bummed out that she had no one left to scold.

CHAPTER 2

Flying to the Mountains

"STOMACH HOLDING UP?" Mama asked. She gave me her concerned-mother look, and put a warm hand to my cheek.

"I'll make it," I said, as my stomach churned and tightened, partly from car sickness, partly from nerves.

We stopped for gas in Plunkit, the last town before Uncle Andrew's. Wedged at the base of the mountains, Plunkit was a depressed and sagging hick town that never seemed to change.

"Comfortable as an old shoe," Mama said fondly of Plunkit.

"Trashy hippies and down-and-out loggers,"

was Grandma Cookie's take on the town.

We turned onto Plunkit Highway and Mama left the speed limit behind, winding smartly around property lines, and then up and up into the remote foothills.

I caught a charge of Mama's energy as we neared her brother's farmhouse. Uncle Andrew stood by the gate, flushed and grinning. We scrambled out of the car to greet him.

"Hey, Bertie!" he boomed to Mama, and trapped her in a bear hug until she squeaked, "Ouch!"

Then he turned to me and said, "How's my favorite niece?"

"I'm you're *only* niece," I said, my standard reply.

He ruffled my hair and pinched my nose. He knew I didn't like getting squeezed.

Uncle Andrew was Mama's little brother, only he wasn't little at all. He was big and bearded, like a Viking. He smelled of coffee, soap, and sawdust from the cabinet shop out back. Andrew was my favorite Uncle. Since my babyhood he had slipped me candy, even when Mama said, "No sweets."

Lately I had lost my taste for candy.

We set our bags in the back bedroom, and then went for lunch in the kitchen, where the woodstove snapped cheerfully. Store-bought flowers and a red checkered tablecloth decorated the round table. Uncle Andrew served alphabet soup because he knew that I liked it. I tried hard to eat it up.

Mama just stared at her coffee. After a while she said, "You know, when I was at Ma's I thought, what the *H* am I going to do now? Really, I didn't have a clue. Then Wil wakes me up from a dead sleep and asks if we can we go to the country."

"It was this weird dream," I tried to explain, "about a tornado, and flying to the mountains."

"I know." Uncle Andrew nodded. "Your Mama told me all about it."

"Well, I don't know why I didn't think of it before," Mama continued. "I mean, leaving the city. Mitch and I were so plugged into the rat race. Me working weekends, and fixing up the darn house. And Mitch working all that overtime, and hating it. I think we just hurried faster and faster so we wouldn't have to deal with each other. Working and squabbling—what a way to live."

"Ahh, Bert. You were doing your best," Uncle Andrew sympathized.

Mama grew teary-eyed. "Our best wasn't good enough," she choked out.

I winced with alarm. It wasn't like Mama to cry. Even Uncle Andrew looked worried over the rare show of emotion. He squeezed her hand nervously. "I think it'll be fun having you two girls here in Hicksville," he said. "Besides, Willa Jane has always liked the country. Remember the ant nest, Wil?"

I remembered it. We had come to Sunday dinner at Uncle Andrew's, and I'd wandered into the woods behind his field. I came upon a waist-high mound crawling with ants.

I watched and I watched, poking the mound with a stick now and then to see what they would do.

I tried to follow where each ant was going. Somewhere in the mound I knew there was a queen, and a hidden nursery filled with eggs, and all these guys were working furiously to serve that queen. How did they know what to do?

Ants would make a good science fair project, and I grew excited at the prospect of charts and graphs and creating an anthill, when Uncle Andrew emerged from the woods. "They're all going ape up at the house, thinking you're lost. Didn't you hear your mama calling?"

"I was just watching these ants. Look at 'em—there's millions!" I answered. I stood still, fascinated by the moving mass that wriggled with purpose.

"You've been out here for two hours, Willa.

Supper's cold and your daddy's walking the creek."

The woods had already grown chilly with the dusk.

"I'm sorry, Uncle Andrew. I was just watching the ants," I whispered, feeling foolish.

"Ahh, that's okay. You can't help yourself. You're a born naturalist, like your uncle." He pointed to his chest with his thumb, like a big bragger. "Now let's get back to the house before they call the marines."

It was true. Animals, clouds, plants, and streams—I did love the outdoors so easily. There was always something fascinating in nature. Always another bend in the stream, or bird in the tree. And if I could be very quiet, or patient, or *aware*, I could see things that others could not.

"I do like being out in the country," I said earnestly.

Uncle Andrew gave me a wink across the table.

"I don't know about you, Roberta, but Willa Jane is going to love it here."

The back bedroom at Uncle Andrew's was dark that night. Dark and quiet, like only the country can be without streetlights or restless cars. Mama and I shared the double bed and I felt snug as a bug under the fluffy down comforter. A faint snort sounded from Mama. I knew she was fast asleep.

At the window a moth fluttered and tapped against the glass, trying in vain to capture the dim glow from the bathroom. Silly moth. Why do they do that?

Now a glow came from outside the window, where a slight figure rested on the sill. One more *tap-tap*. From underneath layers of sleep I heard the moth say, "Welcome, Willa."

CHAPTER 3

Turn Here!

Mama had this plan about renting a nice house in the country, with a little picket fence and roses out front. So after lunch, Uncle Andrew gathered the classifieds and we went house hunting. The three of us climbed into the Workhorse, Uncle Andrew's battered Ford pickup, and we embarked with high hopes to explore the Suquawkle Valley and find that little house with the roses.

We toured a cottage by the river, but Uncle Andrew whispered to Mama that last flood season he'd seen the Suquawkle flowing through its living room. I liked a fancy log home, but Mama clicked her tongue at the price. We got excited over a little farmhouse, but the inside smelled like cat pee, and Mama said she wasn't going to pay rent to smell that smell.

Onward we drove, down winding country roads. My stomach started to tighten with the motion of the truck. I'd have to stop soon or there'd be trouble.

At the side of the road I glimpsed a bright green sign that practically glowed. My stomach lurched menacingly and the landscape wavered. I read the sign. It read PEACE AND COURAGE. On top of the signpost a hand-sized doll was balanced with arms open wide. A passing breeze made the little arms flap a hello.

Startled, I rubbed my eyes and looked again. Now the sign read WICKET'S ROAD, and the doll must have fallen.

"Turn here!" I yelled, compelled by my imagination to follow the "Peace and Courage" road.

Uncle Andrew obeyed and veered sharply off

Plunkit Highway with a skid and a screech.

"Could you stop for a second?" I asked Uncle Andrew.

He pulled over and halted the Workhorse. "I just want to check that sign," I explained, and jumped out, running directly to the post. Quickly I scanned the grass for the doll but found nothing. I reread the sign, which still read WICKET'S ROAD. Puzzled, I returned to the truck.

"Okay, we can go," I said, lost in thought.

With pedal to the metal, Uncle Andrew bombed down the road until Mama smacked him on the shoulder. "Slow down!" she scolded. "Don't drive like a crazy man with my kid in your car."

"Your mother is so *bossy*," Andrew declared, as if he were surprised. He grinned at me, and I rolled my eyes. They often carried on this way, mildly bickering and joking like they were still kids. Andrew braked, and the Workhorse slowed to a respectable speed.

Wicket's Road was a gravel lane carved straight through the woods. The road was so narrow, and the trees that bordered it so immense, that it felt like we were driving through a tunnel of evergreens.

I unrolled my window all the way, breathing in cool, clean air, steadying my stomach. Thinking of the sign with the doll on the top, I wondered if motion sickness could cause mirages, like heatstroke under a desert sun.

Up ahead on the left there was another sign. It read: FOR SALE—HOME IS WHERE THE HEART IS—HART'S REALTY. We pulled into the gravel drive and sat gaping. The house was not a house—it was a *trailer*. And an uglier trailer I could not have imagined.

We spilled out of the truck, and I stretched my legs and wrinkled my nose. "Yuck!" was all I had to say.

"What a dump," Uncle Andrew agreed.

The trailer squatted at the back of a dirt yard

packed hard by feet, hooves, and paws. Proof of the four-legged inhabitants still littered the yard in plentiful, disgusting piles.

And the junk. Rusted car parts, a mildewed sofa, stacks of rotten newspapers, three cracked televisions, assorted lumber pieces—all of it heaped into the yard as if that was where it belonged.

Always practical, Mama said, "Well, since we're here, see if there's an ad in the For Sale section under Hart's Realty."

Uncle Andrew flapped the newspaper. He ran a finger down the columns until he found it, and then he said, "Here it is—'Singlewide mobile on four acres: good well, year-round stream, two tax lots.' Talk about cheap—look at this, Bert." Andrew held the paper for Mama to see.

"Let's take a look," Mama urged. Uncle Andrew and I just stood there.

"Come on," she said, "it won't hurt to look!"

I followed Mama and Uncle Andrew toward the

front porch, stepping cautiously over ancient poop piles. The trailer was an early model with a rounded roof. The color was sort of a moldy green, but something in the eaves was rusting, sending reddish brown streaks down the sides like blood from a wound.

Uncle Andrew rapped at the arched door. It resounded with a hollow echo. With a jiggle he found the door was unlocked.

We were shocked to find that the inside was clean. Someone had tried to paint the interior yellow, but had run out of paint or energy. The yellow stopped short in the hall, where jagged prints of a roller faded away and dark paneling resumed.

It didn't take long to see all there was to see. At the back were two compact bedrooms and a toy-sized bathroom. The living area included an enormous woodstove and a dainty bay that served as a dining area.

"This kitchen is kind of cute," Uncle Andrew

said. "Look at the old fridge, Roberta—right out of the fifties. And the stove isn't half bad."

Mama peeked out the kitchen window. Talking mostly to herself, she said, "I could sell the extra lot if I needed the cash."

We went outside and walked the property. The four acres were really quite impressive once we got away from the yard and trailer. A path led us through the woods, where giant cedars stood with their toes in a winding stream. Miniature waterfalls gushed into green pools. Fallen trees wrapped in moss crisscrossed the stream like fairy bridges. The woods were quiet, and so green the very air appeared tinted.

I had a wild urge to run off like a deer, to follow that stream to see where it led. I liked those woods. I felt as if I belonged there, as if maybe I had been there before.

Reluctantly I followed Mama and Uncle Andrew back to the truck. I was dawdling, enjoying the closeness of the forest, when a light from the ferns caught my eye. A dapple of sunshine? A reflection from a beer can? I could not be sure. I stooped for closer inspection but saw nothing.

Carefully I studied the ground, and as I stared I knew my motion sickness had returned with a vengeance because the air seemed to wobble and glow. Before my eyes, a seedling grew. It formed a bud, and the bud popped open, becoming a snow white trillium. Then, just as quickly, the thing turned brown. It shriveled and withered, and was gone.

Shutting my eyes, I tried to compose myself. When I looked again, there was no flower. Only the memory of the image remained, stark white against green. On a breeze a child's voice hissed, "Show-off."

Suddenly, in a hazy ball of sparkles, a small figure appeared next to where the trillium had sprung. The figure solidified, resembling the doll on the post. Only now the doll could talk.

"I'm no show-off!" she argued. Her hair was

blond and curly, and she was very tan, with a chubby, childish build. "I'm just *talented*," she declared with mischief in her voice, "and you're *jealous*."

As the girl glanced my way her form began to fade. Turning toward an unseen companion, she whispered, "I think she's listening."

The girl and her sparkles disappeared completely. Like the trillium, the incident lasted only seconds. Did it really happen? Was I just tired and sick and imagining these strange little dramas?

I looked intently around the shadowy forest. The trees were wooden giants. The air smelled earthy, like wet stones and old leaves. The stream murmured steadily.

I knew I hadn't been eating or sleeping like I should. I'd felt so rotten lately. Always anxious, or dizzy, or nauseated. No wonder I was making up wacky stories in my head. No wonder my imagination was running wild.

I walked out of the forest and found Mama and

Uncle Andrew at the truck. They were rummaging through a day pack for granola bars and pouring coffee from a thermos. Mama insisted that *she* pour because Uncle Andrew was a "pig." Everything seemed normal.

I mulled over the mirage that I'd just imagined and promised myself to start taking vitamins. When I assessed the woods and the dismal trailer, I was surprised to feel more curious than repelled.

It was strange. As soon as we drove away from that place, I wanted to return.

CHAPTER 4

The Gypsy Wagon

"SO WHAT DID YOU think of Wicket's Road?"
Mama asked. We were in our nighties, getting ready for bed at Uncle Andrew's.

"The yucky trailer? There were definitely no roses."

Mama smiled wryly. "Yeah, it was pretty awful."

"But I liked the property," I admitted. "I liked the property a lot."

"So did I," Mama agreed, and then she sighed. "It would be so much work."

"A *huge* amount of work," I said, nodding.

"But it's so cheap," she countered.

"Cheap for a very good reason," I pointed out.

"It's minutes from Uncle Andrew's. And we do like this area, don't we, Wil?"

"Yeah, we do, Mama."

We got under the covers and Mama turned off the bedside light. "Good night, Willa. Mama loves you." She kissed me as usual, softly on the cheek.

"Hey, Mama?"

"What honey?"

"Did you think that forest was weird or anything?"

"Just big, and peaceful, and very green," Mama answered.

"And growing like crazy," I added. I yawned and mumbled, "A little sparkly, too, like in my dream. Maybe that's why it seemed so familiar."

"Get some sleep, Sweet Pea."

Mama paid cash and the deal closed quickly. In the greenish light of a chilly April morning we stood before our trailer, hardly knowing where to begin.

"Well, I revamped the house in town, didn't I? It looked like *H-E*-double toothpicks before I got my hands on it," Mama bragged. "Besides, renting is for suckers."

With those words of wisdom in my ears I stared dumbly over our new front yard with its layers of filth and mountains of garbage.

Seven loads to the dump and one week later we were finally seeing some progress, thanks to Uncle Andrew and the Workhorse. He brought over his power washer and scoured the entire trailer, careful not to aim too long at any one spot because the jet of water could cut through the old siding like butter.

After a couple of warm days to let the siding dry out, we painted on a white primer that made the trailer gleam. Things were definitely looking up.

Every morning we packed our lunch in Uncle Andrew's kitchen. Mama made coffee, and I made

a big jug of lemon water, which is what I preferred. We ate mostly peanut butter-and-honey
sandwiches, although sometimes Mama splurged
on deli meat. A jumbo bag of Food Warehouse
gingersnaps always accompanied us and strangely
never seemed to diminish.

We lugged our cleaning products and tools in
milk crates and every day we'd add something
new: steel wool, putty knife, crowbar. Then we'd
hit the road, and Mama would play loud rock and
roll on the radio for the short drive down Plunkit
Highway.

I suffered my morning nausea in silence. If I
could keep my breakfast down, the worst would
be over by about nine o'clock. I tried to will myself
to be calm so I wouldn't feel all tense and sick, but
the more I tried, the worse I felt. It wasn't my
heart that got broken over the divorce, it was my
stomach.

During the day we labored so hard that at night
I'd collapse into bed, too weary to think of Daddy,

or the divorce, or my new future, which was a big fat question mark.

At Uncle Andrew's it was comforting to sleep with Mama each night. She would say, "Brush your teeth," and "Good night, Willa, Mama loves you," just as she had always done.

Dear Willa J.,

A quick note between classes. I'm enjoying my courses and learning a lot about computers. I am older than many of the other students, which makes me sort of a dork, but I'm a smart dork.

I wanted to wish you a happy May Day, and I hope you got the flowers that I sent. I miss your little woven paper baskets with the wilted flowers in them. If I think about it too long I will boo-hoo all over my writing.

Mama says you are a good helper

with the trailer project. Sounds like Mama has taken on a lot of work. You keep an eye on each other to make sure you both stay healthy. Your mama works too hard and you forget to eat! I worry about you girls. I'm just glad Uncle Andrew is nearby.

Can you believe it is 85 degrees down here? I'm going swimming every day in that dinky pool of Uncle Jackson's. I'm getting very tan.

Well, I don't have to tell you that I miss you, because you already know. Whenever I get tired of studying, I remind myself that I'd better make the most of this time without my Willa, otherwise it's just time wasted.

Working hard,
Your loving Daddy

I tried to imagine Daddy all tan and going to classes. The only picture I could conjure was from memory: Daddy coming home from work, flipping me upside down and holding me by my feet saying, "Willa, you definitely look different today."

"Those are my feet!" I'd declare with fake exasperation.

"Oh by gosh, you're right!" Daddy would always play a goof to make me laugh.

Though I was eager for his every letter, every letter *bugged* me. There he was, in sunny California, swimming and hanging out with the perfect cousins. Maybe if I were more like Rudy and Zack, Daddy would want to hang out with me. Maybe if I weren't so spaced-out and quiet, Daddy would find me more interesting.

Apparently he preferred college, and the perfect cousins, and a hotter climate, and a different life. Fine with me. My student-Dad seemed un*real*.

The trailer was real. The work was real. Mama did demolition, I did pickup. We ripped, scrubbed, and loaded. We patched, primed, and painted.

Mama seemed tireless, but sometimes I would catch her with this "Oh my God, what have I done?" look on her face. Like when she was determined to replace the wax ring on the toilet. She began to remove the bolts, which were rusted out and crumbling in the grip of her wrench. She got that "What have I done?" look, and started kicking the toilet in frustration. Then she unloaded a string of bad words. I ran outside so I couldn't hear.

It wasn't really the toilet that got her so riled. Mama was dealing with change in her own way, and I think my Mama would rather be mad than sad.

I did all my crying in private so Mama would not know. It seemed like we had to keep our grief to ourselves. As if we could stand only our own portion, and no more.

One day at the Coast to Coast we found twelve gallons of forest green house paint, dirt cheap. Someone had ordered it and never picked it up. We couldn't wait to brush on the gorgeous green and finally make the trailer our own.

The doors and fake shutters we painted a cheerful red. Uncle Andrew made some plant holders for under the kitchen windows; these we painted red also, and filled them with half-price pansies from the Flower Barn.

Satisfied with the exterior, Mama moved indoors, slapping a smooth coat of primer on anything nailed down. White and gleaming, the inside of the trailer looked much larger, and felt fresh and sanitized.

The hard slab of a front yard got pickaxed and rototilled so we could get some grass seed going. I raked, seeded, and watered, and happily watched the tiny sprouts grow and spread into a carpet. The baby grass was soothing, transforming dirt into velvety green.

Mama put me on garden detail, which meant I could create flower beds around the trailer. I used up the half-price pansies and then went "shopping" in our woods, digging for huckleberry, dogwood, salal, and vine maple. I especially liked the ferns with their hairy tentacles uncoiling for springtime, and the groves of lacey filarees with blossoms the color of Pepto-Bismol.

I didn't touch the trilliums. They were in bloom now and behaving as they should. But trilliums are solitary flowers, few and far between, so I didn't feel right disturbing them.

When I was scouting for plants at the back of our property, I entered a patch of clearing that I had not seen before. Setting down my bucket and shovel, I looked around.

The stream slowed to a round pool surrounded by spring grass. A weathered stump rose from one side of the pool. The stump had smooth sides and an irregular top. Of course I had to climb up for a sit.

I settled myself in a comfortable shelf on the queenly stump, and there I rested and dreamed, happy for this moment to be right where I was. The sun was a cool yellow, but it warmed my face if I tilted it toward the light.

Lazily I glanced at the pool. Near the water's edge, hidden in a fern grove, sat a dollhouse. It was fashioned out of sticks and decorated with weathered orange shutters. The little house was dilapidated and covered with moss. It was about the size of a large country mailbox. I slid off the stump to take a closer look, but my foot caught in a crack, and down I tumbled.

Darn! I'd scraped my knee and elbow. Irritated, I looked again for the dollhouse, but it seemed to be gone. I searched through every fern in the clearing, but the little house had vanished.

Had I fallen asleep and dreamed of the dollhouse?

Or was some neighbor kid playing tricks on me?

I recalled my "mirage" of the sparkling girl in the woods. At about four inches tall, she was just the right size for that little stick house. The back of my neck went prickly with the oddness of it all.

A distinct sensation swept over me. It was the feeling that someone or something was watching me. Gathering my shovel and bucket, I left the clearing and hurried home.

At the trailer, Mama was putting down linoleum tile. I stood in the doorway and observed as she spread some thick glue onto the floor with a metal comb.

"Hey, Mama—did the people who lived here before us have any kids?" I asked.

"The realtor said they were grown and gone," Mama answered without looking up.

"Well, did they have any grandchildren?"

"Never heard."

"Do you think there could be—oh, I don't

know—bad guys in the woods?" I asked nonchalantly.

Mama looked up sharply, then answered, "I think we're pretty safe and sound here Willa—something bothering you?"

"No, I'm not bothered. It's just, well, our woods seem a little funny, that's all." I waited to see what Mama would say to that.

Putting down her tool and stretching her back, Mama surprised me with what she said next.

"I think our woods are funny, too. Sometimes I feel they are so old and quiet that the spirits of the Indians or pioneers must be out there. Is that what you mean by funny?"

"Yeah, I guess that's what I mean—something like that."

"Are you scared of the woods, Wil?" Mama wiped adhesive from her hands and eyed me with her penetrating stare.

I thought for a long moment. "I'm not afraid, just—I don't know. I thought I saw this dollhouse in the woods, and the next minute it was gone. It was weird, and got me to thinking about being watched."

Mama's face turned tense, and somehow I knew she was worrying about my health again. Maybe this time thinking I was cracking up.

"I must have fallen asleep on that stump and had a dream is all," I said quickly.

A hefty engine growl alerted us to company. I turned to see the Workhorse gliding into the driveway with Uncle Andrew at the wheel. From the seat of his truck he produced a white pizza box, and in a bad Italian accent he boomed, "Who order da pizza pie?"

Mama laughed and rolled her eyes. "Do I have to pay for da pizza pie?" she yelled. Mama had become a tightwad.

"It's-a my treat!" sang the Italian Andrew.

Sidetracked by Uncle Andrew, Mama did not return to the conversation about our mysterious woods. But the feeling of being watched lingered, and I kept picturing the mossy-roofed dollhouse with the weathered orange shutters. The picture had been so clear, and the dream had seemed so real.

On Saturday we drove the Workhorse into the city to get clothes from Grandma Cookie's and some furniture out of storage. Mama was strict about what we brought, since our new home was so snug it wouldn't take much to furnish it.

I was glad to get back to the country again. Springtime's new growth had thatched the roof of the Wicket's Road "tunnel" so the sun could only peek through in spots and speckles. The road had a cozy feel.

As we bumped along I pretended I'd never been down the road before. And then, look! There to the left. A darling place, freshly painted green, with cheerful red shutters, surrounded by ferns and flowers.

We pulled into the driveway and jerked to a stop.

"Well, we're home," Mama said, like it was an important statement to make.

"I think it looks like a gypsy house," I mused.

"A gypsy *wagon*," corrected Mama.

The Gypsy Wagon it became.

CHAPTER 5

Hazel Wicket

"ARE WE POOR?" I asked Mama one morning as she noisily rustled the local paper assessing the want ads.

"Poorer than some, richer than others," Mama answered vaguely.

May had turned warm as we put the final touches on the Gypsy Wagon and got all moved in. Our first morning we sat at the dining nook; Mama drank her black coffee, and I played with my cereal.

Mama glanced my way. "Quit playing and start eating," she ordered.

The radio hummed softly in our sparkling

kitchen. We had brought a small TV but discovered it had no reception. It was radio or nothing.

"So, *are* we, Mama?" I persisted.

"Are we what?"

"Are we *poor*?"

In the past money had never seemed like a concern, but since the divorce I'd become aware of prices and budgets and bargains. When Mama and I went to Plunkit Wise Deal, I'd scan the aisles calculating cost—low, lower, and lowest. I'd added money to my list of worries.

Dropping her newspaper, Mama glared at me with serious brows. She folded the paper and set it on the table.

"Well, we have to watch our budget," she said matter-of-factly. "And I have to get a job. But we can manage. We got a fat chunk of money from the house in town, and I paid cash for the Gypsy Wagon. We own it free and clear—and we still have money in the bank. Now you let me do the worrying. I'm better at it than you are."

"All right, Mama."

But it wasn't all right. The butterflies in my stomach stirred. Could Mama get a job, and who would watch me if she did? When would Daddy come for visits? And school would start eventually. I couldn't even think about a new school. Life had gotten so worrisome.

From the front door came a resounding *bang-bang-bang!* Mama and I nearly fell out of our chairs, we were so startled. We scrambled to the living room, expecting our regular visitor, Uncle Andrew. Instead Mama opened the door to an old woman bearing a pie. It took us several moments to adjust to this unlikely company.

"Uhh, can I help you?" Mama asked.

"I'm your neighbor up the road—Hazel Wicket." She balanced the pie on one hand and offered a veiny hand to shake. "I brought you this pie to welcome you to the neighborhood! I would have come sooner, but I could see you were busy around here," she said, regarding the trailer approvingly.

Despite her powerful knock, Mrs. Wicket spoke softly and had a shy smile. She was a petite woman with hunched-over shoulders. A tight bun gathered her frosty hair at the nape of her neck, and wrinkles textured every inch of her skin. She was definitely *o-l-d*, old.

"May I take that for you?" I asked, remembering my manners, and looking at the skinny arms holding the humungous pie.

"Thank you," Mrs. Wicket said, and she smiled at me with kind eyes.

Ushering Mrs. Wicket inside, Mama offered to cut the pie right then, but Mrs. Wicket said we should save it for dessert.

"Will you have a cup of coffee, Mrs. Wicket?" Mama seemed excited to have a guest who wasn't her brother.

"I would love some."

Mrs. Wicket sat down, smoothing her apron. It was a bib style with huge pockets. Under the apron she wore a gray blouse and a faded black skirt that went almost to her ankles. Black, masculine shoes could not disguise her tiny feet. The outfit was old-fashioned but dignified. She took her coffee with lots of milk, and sipped it with prim, tidy movements.

I noticed a chunky, wooden walking stick tucked beneath Mrs. Wicket's arm. No doubt it had been the stick doing the banging, and not our soft-spoken neighbor.

Mama introduced us as "Roberta Northup, and my daughter, Willa Mackenzie." Mama wanted her old name back, and would be legally changing it. I would still be a Mackenzie, since that was the name I was born with.

Hearing the names said out loud made me cringe. I felt a sense of embarrassment at being different from the average family. We now seemed messy, complicated, and in need of some explanation that I didn't want to give.

Mrs. Wicket said politely, "Everything looks

real good. You have done wonders with this place!"

"Thank you." Mama beamed. "It was a big job. My brother helped us quite a bit," she conceded.

"Mrs. Wicket," I asked, "were you named after this road?" I realized too late that it was probably a dumb question.

"Actually, the road was named after me—my family, that is." She smiled and explained. "My dad settled in these parts before there even was a Plunkit. His name was Henry Cole. I grew up in the house that he built, and that is my house today."

"But wouldn't that make it Cole's Road?" I asked.

"It was known as Cole's Road around here for a long time, but not on the maps, just by us locals. As my dad got older, he thought to move to town. Mr. Wicket and I were living up out of Monroe in those years, but we returned to rent the old home place from dad. When my father died the house and property became ours. So, since the mid-thirties this has been Wicket's Road, and it's Wicket's Road on the maps," she finished proudly.

Mama ran to the kitchen to dig out the never-ending gingersnaps and she hurriedly dumped some on a pretty plate.

"Gingersnap?" Mama offered.

"Don't mind if I do," said Mrs. Wicket.

The conversation drifted to grown-up interests like property prices and taxes. Bored, I stealthily made my way toward my bedroom.

I had claimed the smallest room, which Mama had painted sky blue. Then together we'd sponged puffy white clouds all over the walls and ceiling. Daisies covered my bed, and hung at the windows—fabric that Mama found at Saint Vincent's in Monroe. My dresser was painted white, along with my old wicker tea chair and the matching mirror. These days I despised that mirror; it showed me as such a scrawny, ugly thing. I stuck my tongue out at my reflection and flopped wearily onto my bed.

Dear Willa Wonka,

Did you get the shells I sent? We found them on the beach last Saturday. I thought you would like the dark one with the wave pattern on it.

I started tending bar at Antonio's (good tips) four nights a week. My classes have gotten very demanding. Am I tired! I can't go without sleep like these young kids can. When I was their age I went without sleep, only it was because of you!

Your mama and I had you when we were nineteen. I remember when you were about seven months old and you got this nasty cold. Your poor little head was filled up with snot. Mama had walked you for two nights, and she said it was my turn or she would go cuckoo.

So I squeezed you into the front pack, and we sat in the rocker and watched <u>The Late Show</u> and <u>Nightmare Theater</u>. Well, I watched, and you dozed. Believe it or not I enjoyed that night—just me and my girl.

Even though we're apart right now, you are still my little girl.

Love,
Daddy

I swept Daddy's letter off the bedspread. I didn't know what to think. My feelings were big and swirling, like that dream tornado. I suspected it was Mama who'd called it quits on the marriage, but it was Daddy who'd left in short order, pursuing his dream, getting tan in his brother's pool, hanging out with his brother's children. All of it, without *me*.

"Come here, Ratty-Monkey." I hugged my oldest stuffed animal, a threadbare sock monkey with no tail.

"Poor old Ratty," I whispered.

I must have dozed off until I heard my name mentioned. Once my snoop antenna was alerted I could not relax. Edging closer to the door, I listened to Mama and Mrs. Wicket.

"Willa took it hard," Mama said in a hushed tone. "She's been a wreck since Mitch and I broke up. It's the stomach thing that worries me. She eats like a bird and she's nauseated half the time. And she doesn't sleep worth a darn. You saw her—she looks like a ghost." Mama paused, sucking in a ragged breath.

"I feel so guilty," she squeaked. "I mean, dragging Willa through all this. She's such a sensitive kid. It was just that Mitch and I married so young, and we grew into different people. We were bringing out the worst in each other. Well, it's over—it's done." Sniffing and nose blowing followed.

"Now, now," a voice said soothingly. "You are a good mother. Your little girl will heal in time. Don't you fret—there, there."

Peeking out of my doorway, I spied Mrs. Wicket leaning over Mama. Her small hand patted Mama gently on the back.

Mama gathered herself and said, "I thought we could find a fresh start out here. I could run a little shop, and Willa could commune with nature the way she likes. We could make a nice niche for ourselves. But sometimes I think I've just screwed everything up." Mama dabbed at her eyes with a hankie.

"You're moving on—that's all you can do," Mrs. Wicket said. "And it's hard to be on your own— don't I know it. But, Roberta, you will find the right road. Just keep on being strong and good."

"I try," answered a childlike voice that was Mama's.

I crept back into my room and looked in the

mirror, repeating Mama's words: "You saw her—she looks like a ghost."

I groaned and shook my head tiredly. Why, Mama knew exactly what was going on with me. I had not fooled her one little bit. And she wasn't fooling me, either. Mama was not as tough as she made out.

CHAPTER 6

Voodoo Creek

"HOT DOG! THIS IS right up my alley," Mama exclaimed. She'd spotted an ad in the *Suquawkle Banner* for help wanted at Plunkit Used Books. Back in the city Mama had worked weekends at Schwartz Books for as long as I could remember. She was casual when she said, "Let's take a little drive to town," but her jaw was set.

Across from Good Junk Antiques, next to The Bad Boy Café, Plunkit Used Books sat at the corner looking tired and faded. Weather and time had scraped most of the paint off the building, including a scratchy sign over the doorway that read: PLUNKIT US BOO . It was pitiful.

Inside, our noses received an immediate impression of dust and neglect. This didn't stop Mama, who plowed ahead, asking for the manager.

"I'm not the manager but I might as well be," said a plump and beautiful black woman behind the counter. "I'm Vivian." She flashed us a toothpaste smile. "Lazy old Herb Moss is the owner and supposed manager, but we don't see him much around here. I finally got his royal permission to hire someone for weekends—plus Monday and Tuesday—so I can go home once in a while. Gretchen is in and out, but she's mostly a buyer."

Vivian seemed happy to be talking to someone about the irritating Mr. Moss and his poorly managed bookstore. I slipped away to wander the aisles while Mama and Vivian chatted.

The space was cavernous, divided into aisles by rows of mismatched bookshelves. Books were everywhere—squeezed into shelves, scattered on tables, stacked on the floor. An old-paper smell saturated the air. In a sunbeam I saw dust suspended in a cloud so thick that I tried breathing through the collar of my shirt like a mask.

I sneezed a big, wet sneeze, which brought my eyes to rest on a booklet put out by the Suquawkle Historical Society—"Plunk It Down and Rest a Spell: A Local History of Plunkit." I paged absently through the paperback until I saw the word *Wicket*. With growing interest, I sat down and read:

Hazel and Jack Wicket, one of Plunkit's oldest families, resided on Wicket's Road, just off the Old Plunkit Highway. Hazel and Jack inherited the 40-acre homestead from Hazel's father, the respected Henry J. Cole, a Plunkit pioneer who helped settle the Suquawkle Valley. Cole's Dry Goods was one of the earliest businesses in Plunkit, operating until the proprietor's death in 1936. (See Downtown Plunkit, p. 24.) Cole's 40 acres was entrenched in local legend for strange phenomena. (See Little Voodoo Creek, p. 14.)

My neck tingled at the words. I hurriedly flipped the pages and read on:

Little Voodoo Creek was named by woodsmen and trappers for odd happenings and strange phenomena rumored to occur in the vicinity of this otherwise unremarkable waterway.

One documented tale of mystery appeared in the *Suquawkle Banner* in 1899, when a local hunting enthusiast made camp on Little Voodoo only to awaken to a vandalized campsite. No real harm had been done, but his gun was missing. Outraged, the hunter was sure he had been robbed, until he returned home to Plunkit later that day. His wife was baffled as to why he had sneaked home the previous afternoon and thrown his gun down the privy hole.

What made the story newsworthy was that the hunter had been Plunkit's own mayor, Arthur Bentley, respected businessman and civic leader. Bentley claimed he had stowed his gun safely in the tent at about 5:00 P.M. He had some grub, read until dark, and then called it a day.

Mrs. Bentley claimed she had noticed the gun in the hole at about 5:30 P.M., when she had been "visiting the premises." She recalled the time precisely, she remembered, because she was timing a cake in the oven.

In those days of bum roads and horse and wagon, traversing the mileage in a half hour was simply impossible. Despite whispers of drink, jokes about mental instability, and years of teasing by locals, Mr. and Mrs. Bentley stuck by their stories. It is interesting to note that in native jargon the area was known as "Kloshe Tenas-Tillicum Chuck," which translates as "Happy Little-People Creek."

I carried the booklet up to the counter and asked Mama if we could buy it. Vivian interrupted, saying, "Honey, it's yours, my compliments."

Mama took the job. She would start Saturday, which posed the problem of what to do with me. I told Mama I'd go crazy sitting around the bookstore all day because it was so dingy. I was immediately sorry I'd said this because then I pictured Mama, stuck in the bookstore all day, trying to make her measly wage.

To celebrate the new job, Mama and I went over to the Bad Boy for milk shakes. The Bad Boy was decorated with lots of chrome and red Formica. The signs advertised really old stuff, like some kind of soda called Bubble Up.

"This is a good deal for me, Wil, just you wait

and see." Mama smiled like she knew something I didn't. "You might think I'm taking a lemon of a job, but I'll make lemonade out of it if it kills me." She sucked up the last of her shake noisily and added, "I've got lots of ideas, Wil. Lots of ideas."

Since I was too young to stay at home alone all day or hang around town, we'd have to rely on Uncle Andrew until we could figure out something else. Then "something else" came knocking at our door, again.

CHAPTER 7

The End of the Road

"I'M NO SPRING CHICKEN, that's for sure. All the chores up at my house are getting away from me," Mrs. Wicket sighed. "Can't keep my head screwed on with all the work. You know, if I had a girl to give me a hand this summer, I'd go easier."

Mrs. Wicket's eyes flicked my way. She had appeared early at our doorstep asking if she'd left her walking stick behind, which she had.

"I'm up a creek myself," Mama said, falling into the country lingo. "I took a job at the bookstore in town, but I don't have a sitter for Willa. Say, maybe we could help each other out?"

"How's that?" Hazel asked.

"Well, I'm thinking a trade of some sort," Mama said brightly.

"That's an idea." Hazel beamed.

They both looked at *me*.

"Willa, would you and your mama like to walk me back to my house, and maybe take a look around?" Mrs. Wicket asked with enthusiasm.

"Well, okay," I agreed hesitantly. I smelled a setup.

The three of us walked at a snail's pace up the road. Mrs. Wicket stepped carefully to avoid pits and pebbles; first the walking stick crept forward, then the sensible shoes followed, step after cautious step.

Wicket's Road narrowed to a wagon path lined by apple trees, soft and fluffy-looking in their spring bonnets. Petals snowed on us with the occasional breeze.

To the left was forest. To the right, a field rambled into the distance. It was bordered by rotting fences that were smothered in wild roses. Dotting the field were apple trees perched here and there above the tall grass. Birds swooped busily, and a deer came into view.

We approached a circular turnaround. There, the forest opened, revealing a large, flourishing garden with an artistic stick bench at the far end.

"Holy cow!" exclaimed Mama. "That garden is a month ahead of the whole valley." Hazel's crops were high and bursting with health. "You've got some kind of green thumb," Mama complimented her.

"I do like my garden," Hazel said.

Nearby, chickens clucked softly from a coop and pen. They were of the "Little Red Hen" variety, looking picturesque pecking their grain in the morning sun.

Under a rickety carport sat a wide, gleaming car. It was a turquoise color, trimmed in shining chrome.

"That thing still run?" Mama asked.

"Like a charm," Hazel answered. "Guzzles the

gas but it gets me there."

Opposite the garden, a well-trodden path pointed lazily to Mrs. Wicket's front porch. On it sat a single rocker and a big yellow cat. The cat was sprawled on a nubby mat that read WELCOME FRIENDS. Honeysuckle wrapped up the front porch and wound around the chimney. The house struck me as sweet as a country calendar cover.

"Your place can't get much cuter," Mama said.

Scattered around the big yard was a hodge-podge of outbuildings, including one rose-tangled shack with a crescent moon on the door. An out-house in this day and age? I wondered.

All the structures suffered from weather and rot. But honeysuckle, wisteria, and the wild roses helped to prop up the homestead and keep it all standing. The property was shabby but neat as a pin, like Mrs. Wicket herself.

"Look at all those birds, Wil." Mama was point-ing to the spreading maple that shaded the south side of the house. In the tree were bird feeders of all shapes and sizes, hanging like Christmas ornaments. The easy snacks lured every kind of bird, and they seemed to be politely taking turns at the feeders.

Flowery scents wafted by. I breathed deeply and felt drowsy and calm. There was a peace about this place that sort of cradled me. It was a peace that came from age, nature, quiet, the end of the road.

"I like your property, Mrs. Wicket," I said.

"Please call me Hazel." She lifted a hand above her eyes as a sunshade, and surveyed her garden, the field, and the birds at the feeders.

"I like my property, too," she said.

Over mint tea in Hazel's kitchen it was decided that Hazel would watch me for the summer in return for help with her chores. I soon discovered her chores were numerous and hard. The Wickets had never bothered to hook up to electricity, or running water, or even a flush system.

Water was pumped by hand in the well house, then hauled to the kitchen in tin pails. It was slow going for someone Hazel's age, but she claimed it kept her fit.

No electricity meant kerosene lamps for light and a woodstove for heat. Hazel ordered cordwood once a year, split and stacked. A local boy chopped kindling weekly. There was a propane stove and a refrigerator in the kitchen; propane and the automobile were Hazel's only concessions to technology.

The door with the crescent moon did indeed hide a toilet.

"If you have to go number two, sprinkle a little ash down the hole when you're finished. Keeps the backhouse fresh," Hazel instructed, winking.

When I went to use the outhouse I found the inside was whitewashed and clean. The only accessories were a roll of toilet paper, a flyswatter, and the "spider stick."

The spider stick was to give the hole a stir

before sitting down—"in case any bugs are hiding in the hole or under the rim of the seat," Hazel had explained. Terrified, I stirred the hole with vigor and paranoia.

I was amazed. It never occurred to me that someone could live like this in modern times. Yet Hazel seemed at peace with her existence.

"I like to keep my place clean and simple," Hazel stated.

"But, Hazel, wouldn't it be simpler to turn on a faucet or switch on a light?" I asked, shocked at Hazel's logic.

Hazel just smiled and answered, "Those things come at a cost—money, noise, and ruckus."

I assumed that Hazel meant she was too poor to afford improvements and was sorry I'd asked. Then Hazel added, "To get those conveniences I'd have to bring in bulldozers and backhoes, smoke and noise!" Hazel paused as if contemplating that horrible possibility.

"No." She shook her head, determined. "We

like it clean and quiet here. That's why we live at the end of the road."

"We" meant Hazel and her big yellow cat Ol' Cougar, who was now dozing on an overstuffed armchair in the front room. I smiled at Ol' Cougar, who unlike his name, looked about as fierce as a fat, sleepy baby.

Walking home from Hazel's, Mama sighed a big sigh, and mostly to herself said, "I do believe we are on the right road."

"And I do believe I've been railroaded," I commented.

Mama looked at me with exaggerated shocked brows. Then she smiled.

"Smart kid," she admitted.

CHAPTER 8

Tales of the Nutfolk

D ARN STOMACH. I had been too nervous to eat breakfast so my insides felt worse than usual. It was Mama's first day of work, and my first day at being a "helper."

Hazel met us on the porch, and after the schedule was understood, she waved Mama away with a firm "Don't you worry about a thing. We'll see you around five thirty. Go on now!"

Reluctantly Mama left with her "I must be brave" look plastered on her face.

"I'll be fine, Mama! You have a good day at work," I called after her. My stomach twisted, belying the "happy kid" look fixed on my face.

"Come and have some breakfast. I'll bet you didn't eat with all the hurry-up and rush." Hazel guided me into the kitchen and sat me in front of a bowl of oatmeal with brown sugar. Hot cocoa steamed in a mug. Hazel asked me how I preferred my eggs.

"I like them very, very dry and scrambled," I answered, knowing full well that adults were incapable of cooking eggs the way I liked them.

"Not slimy, eh?" Hazel acknowledged. She whipped the eggs with a fork and cooked them just right.

I ate pretty good for me.

Saturday was general cleanup day. Hazel's house was easy to clean because it was so sparse and organized. Five rooms and no piles or clutter.

I had trouble remembering that there were no lights to switch on, and no faucets to bring water. The bathroom had a sink and a tub, but the hot and cold fixtures were mere decorations. Bath and sink water drained into a "gray water" pool down by the blackberries, so Hazel was careful to use only mild soaps.

A Port-A-Pottie sat in the bathroom corner, "For emergencies only," Hazel instructed. I was about to ask "What emergencies?" when I sort of figured it out for myself.

A narrow staircase went upstairs from the front room. "I don't bother with the upstairs much since the kids have gone," Hazel said. She hustled away to look for furniture polish before I could glean more information about "the kids."

I was dusting in the front room when my eyes rested on a painting that hung above the desk. The painting was of a forest scene, with a large stump and a green pool in the foreground. The light suggested sunset, with golden tints and deep shadows.

At first I thought it was the stump on our property, but the shape wasn't right. This stump was tall and wide. Some long-ago disaster had snapped the massive tree maybe six feet up. But the wood looked free of rot, and the roots still clung to the earth in thick, solid ropes.

Looking closer, I saw dots of tiny violets blooming around the pond. The whole scene was too pretty to be real. In a margin the artist had titled it in neat letters: BEHIND NATURE'S MAGIC. To the right was scrawled *Rachel Meeker*.

"I sure like this picture!" I called out to Hazel in the kitchen.

"What picture is that?"

"The one with the stump in the forest."

Hazel appeared in the foyer. "Isn't that a beaut? The artist was my good friend and neighbor. She's gone now, died of cancer last summer. I think if the house was afire, that painting would be one of the few things I'd be sure to haul out."

"Do you think it's worth a lot?"

"Only to me," Hazel said.

I dusted, polished, swept, and mopped. Then I noticed that I was actually hungry.

"Hazel, should we have some lunch?" I hinted.

My interest in food sent Hazel immediately to the kitchen. She started banging around in there like company was coming. Not ten minutes later I was sitting down to grilled cheese on white bread, tomato soup, sliced apples, and chocolate cake for desert. A glass of milk and some mint tea topped it off. Hazel regarded me with satisfaction as I ate.

After lunch we needed water from the well to wash dishes. I headed to the well house, eager to try the old-fashioned pump. After a few squeaky thrusts on the handle, water began spitting, then rushing into my pail.

Next we had to heat the water, so I poured it into a large canning pan on the back burner of the stove. When the water was hot, we dumped it into the faucetless sink, which contained one plastic tub for wash water, another for the rinse. Hazel washed and I dried. Our chores were done.

"Nap time," Hazel announced.

"Hazel, I'm ten years old. I don't really take naps anymore."

"Not your nap time—*my* nap time," Hazel replied with a smirk.

"Oh," I said sheepishly.

"But if you want to relax a bit, you can snuggle on the bed and I'll tell you a story. I like to nap in my rocker," Hazel said.

I had the suspicious feeling that I was being tricked, but I liked the idea of a story. So, shoes off, I snuggled down into Hazel's bed. It smelled faintly of lavender and bleach. She pulled up the rocker and tossed an afghan over her knees. Hazel had a pleasant voice for storytelling. I listened as she began her tale of May Pocket:

Long ago there was a little girl named May Pocket. She lived with her folks in a clapboard house in the

woods, back in the olden days. She
was a curious girl, and loved the nat-
ural world. May liked to wander
through the woods around her house,
discovering things of interest: plants,
creatures, streams, rocks and such—

"That sounds like me!" I broke in.

"May was a lot like you, Willa." Hazel looked thoughtful. "You two could have been sisters."

Because May was a happy child,
she could enjoy all she experienced,
and she could experience all she
enjoyed.

"Do you know what I mean?" Hazel interrupted herself.

I repeated slowly, "'She could enjoy all she experienced, and she could experience all she enjoyed. I know what you mean—it's like filling your head with where you're at."

"That's right." Hazel smiled approvingly, then continued:

> One day May came across something interesting. It was a great old stump with twisty roots that made caves and cubbies at the base. The stump sat near a pond with tiny violets creeping to the water's edge. May was enchanted, and sat down to observe, as was her custom.

"Like the one in the painting," I blurted.

"Just like that one," Hazel answered, and then she went on:

> May sat quiet and peaceful, closing her eyes and turning her face to the sun. Summer was glorious, her chores were done, and life was good.

Opening her eyes, May was shocked to see that the entire picture had changed. Oh, the stump was still there and the violets, too, but there was more—much more than May had detected a moment ago!

A tiny village had appeared around the pond, and the stump was clearly a dwelling, with windows, shutters, doors, and balconies. People were busy here and there— small people, not much bigger than May's hand. May just stared and stared.

WELCOME said a miniature sign TO NUTFOLK WOOD, POPULATION 52.

Hazel's words gave me that tingly feeling. This story of a dreamy girl, a stump, and a tiny village brought back the image of the dollhouse in my woods, and the sparkly girl who could have lived in it. I must have been dreaming, I thought. And Hazel's story is just a coincidence.

May rubbed her eyes, and checked her forehead for fever. Then she pinched her arm using her fingernails, just in case she might be sleeping.

But May was not sleeping. Wide awake and quite present, she had stumbled upon something incredible. By chance or fate she had wandered into the midst of a mystical village inhabited by fairies. Not the winged fairies of storybooks. Not the trick-sters of European lore, but something else. They were hearty creatures: sensitive, kind, and productive. They were human in their nature, and English in their language. They were of a little-known branch of fairies called the Nutfolk.

May could not believe her luck, or her eyes, to have fairies in her own backyard! That night in bed May doubted her own sanity. But in the light of day she saw the Nutfolk again, and again.

In the beginning May only observed, respectfully and from a distance. Eventually, though, she befriended some Nutfolk, and learned their customs and their ways. Ah, but that's a tale for another day.

Hazel stopped her storytelling and was looking drowsy. I was eager to hear more, but Hazel said, "That's all for now. I think I'll just catch forty winks." And with that Hazel closed her eyes, still smiling a little smile.

I couldn't argue with a tired old lady, so I lay back and thought about her story, with no intention of falling asleep.

I dreamed of little people, and stump homes. A tiny girl in an acorn cap and a fringed, Indian-like jacket whispered in my ear, "Be happy, Willa Jane."

"I can't—because of the divorce," I stammered.

"What's a divorce?" the nutgirl asked.

I struggled to explain. "A divorce is when everything changes."

"Change is hard," the girl agreed, "until change becomes the day."

Perplexed, I turned to ask her what she meant, but she had gone. I blinked, confused at the sight of fluffy white hills. Then the hills solidified into Hazel's feather pillows.

I awoke to the clamor of pots and pans clanking in the kitchen. Hazel must have gotten up and gotten busy. When I padded in sock feet to the kitchen, Hazel handed me some shears and said, "Get your shoes on and go pick us some pretty flowers," which I did.

At five thirty sharp, Mama was at the door to pick me up. Hazel was scrubbing the stove, and I was sketching flowers at the kitchen table. Mama looked pleased to hear about the nice lunch I had eaten, and the nap I had taken. Hazel made a big deal about what a good helper I was, which was embarrassing but true.

Once we were out the door, Mama drew me near and asked, "Well, how'd it go?" so if I had rotten things to say about Hazel I could say them freely. But I put her fears to rest.

"Hazel is really old, but she's okay. And her house is okay. And her cat is okay. And her cooking is better than okay."

Laughing, Mama kissed my cheek loudly and said, "You're okay yourself."

CHAPTER 9

A Tough Row to Hoe

SUNDAY MORNING I WALKED alone to Hazel's house. The road was pink with petals and the air smelled like springtime. A venerable lilac had burst into lavender next to a flowering quince. Wild honeysuckle was creeping up Douglas firs and maples, trying to get their share of the sun.

Was there a prettier spot than this? If so, I didn't need it.

I found Hazel in the kitchen frying bacon and flipping pancakes. Biscuits were warming in the oven and coffee perked on the stove.

I did a double take at the bountiful breakfast,

pained that Hazel had gone to so much trouble when I'd already eaten.

"Gee, Hazel, I ate some cereal this morning," I confessed, "and I don't think I'm hungry for all this."

Hazel chuckled. "This isn't for you. This is for my woodcutter. He chops all my kindling for the week and keeps my grass cut. There he is!" Hazel pointed a finger toward the kitchen window.

A skinny, dark-haired boy in a shabby denim jacket appeared out of the woods to the north. Gracefully he vaulted the fence with his hand on the top rail and an effortless spring of his legs to the side.

I spied on him as he neared the porch. He had a mean look—sort of tough and sullen. He was pale in complexion with a narrow chin and a straight, pointed nose. His eyes were dark, bordered with long black lashes. His hair was scraggly and uncombed.

When he reached the porch he smiled, like he'd

been saving up that smile just for Hazel. He showed white teeth and dimples and looked suddenly like a nice kid instead of a delinquent.

"Hey! You'd better have a big stack, 'cause I'm hungry!" the boy bellowed cheerfully. He stomped dirt off his feet at the mat, and when he entered he smelled like the outdoors.

Hazel stepped forward and introduced us. "This is Willa Mackenzie. She'll be helping with my housework this summer. And Willa, this is Vincent Meeker, my all-around handyman."

Vincent glared at me. He grunted a "Hey," then scraped a chair back and slumped at the table. I figured he was older than me but he wasn't acting like it.

"Hi, Vincent," I said shyly.

The moment stretched like taffy, and with no response from Vincent. I added lamely, "I guess I'll go get some water." I escaped the moody kitchen and hurried to the well house.

After I had wasted as much time as possible

dinking around at the pump, I walked slowly back to the kitchen. My plan was to start the dishes, and to ignore Vincent Meeker.

At the table, Vincent and Hazel were laughing over some joke. I don't know what Hazel said to Vincent while I was gone, but he had changed his tune.

He cleared his throat and said, "I saw what you guys did to that dump of a trailer. I've been checking it out. Sure looks nice."

"Well, thanks."

"It must have been a heck of a lot o' work." Vincent was straining to make conversation.

"Yeah, it was pretty hard, but we just kept at it," I answered.

"I really like how you painted it, and put the plants around and everything."

"That was me. I mean, I did all the flower beds," I said, thinking as I spoke that I sounded like a bragger.

"Your trailer reminds me of this old painting I

saw in a book," Vincent said thoughtfully. "You should pick a bunch of flowers and sit on the porch, and have your Mom take a picture. That would make a really good picture." Vincent stared out the window but I was sure he was seeing the image he'd just described.

I was surprised at his artistic suggestion. He turned to see me gaping at him, and slowly his cheeks and ears began to flush a rosy pink.

"Hazel, how about some more coffee?" Vincent blustered.

"You better have another cup," Hazel warned. "You see that grass? Grew almost a foot since last week. And I need the wood bin full; these mornings are still cool. And you said you'd sharpen those mower blades."

"What would you do without me?" Vincent teased.

"Guess I'd be up that creek without a paddle," Hazel replied, grinning.

I'd never seen a kid drink coffee, but Vincent

downed it like soda. He finished his cup, scraped back his chair, and took his plate to the sink. "I better get to it. Nice meetin' you, Willa," he said courteously. He banged the screen door loudly on the way out.

Hazel rolled her eyes. "Boys!" she said happily.

We washed the breakfast dishes, then Hazel got her shawl from the hook by the door. "Sunday is walk day," she announced. "Let's go."

Vincent rattled by with a manual push mower, cutting neat roads in the grass.

"Why is Sunday walk day, Hazel?" I asked as we strolled behind the house on a trail to the woods.

"Well, for some folks Sunday is a day of worship. For others it's a day of rest. And some people like to spend Sundays with friends and family. When I'm walking the property, I can do all of that." Hazel smiled a sad and distant smile.

The day was picture perfect, with wispy clouds in a mellow blue sky. Hazel showed me trails she had roamed as a girl. We passed the beaver ponds, and meandered through a grove of tall cedars. Then we stepped into an open field; it smelled sweet with warm grass and wild roses. We didn't talk much, just walked.

We looped around south and caught the road back to the house. Hazel toured her garden, exclaiming over corn, cabbage, and onions like they were old friends.

"Spinach looks good, but those radishes seem a little yellow. I got sweet peas coming up over here, just for pretty."

The garden was spectacular—as tidy and lush as a picture in a magazine. It didn't look quite real in its perfection with green rows stretching for fifty feet, ending at the foot of the wooden bench that looked more like art than furniture. It was built out of unusual twigs and sticks with fantastic curlicues and lumpy knots. "Did you build that bench, Hazel?"

"Heavens no. Mr. Wicket was quite a carpenter.

An artist, really." Hazel beamed proudly.

"Look at that little feller," she said, changing the subject. Hazel was pointing to a gray rabbit on the other side of the fence. She pulled a few carrot nibs and tossed them his way. "Now take a hike," she said sternly.

We followed the trail behind the carport that led to Little Voodoo Creek. We came upon a rustic bridge with a log handrail. Hazel motioned to a bench in the same twig style. "I think I'll just rest and contemplate a spell," she said, and sat down with a heavy sigh.

I wondered if she was contemplating or sleeping, but I was happy to snoop around the creek. I crossed the bridge back and forth a few times and jumped to test its strength. Then I leaned over and spit in the water.

Not far past the bridge, the channel dropped, causing a slight waterfall. I settled into a game of sending leaves over the falls, watching them land and swirl in the pool below.

A small sound met my ears, carried on the whims of air currents. It was like chickens arguing, or children playing. I strained to hear more, turning this way and that like a radar dish, attempting to pinpoint direction. As I followed the stream around the bend, the noise became clearer.

The sounds seemed to center around a second pool in the stream, deeper and larger than the one by the bridge. It was edged with round rocks and boulders, making a nifty little swim hole.

Laughter and a flurry of tiny voices rose. "Look out below!" called an unseen diver, and something went *plunk* in the pool. Then came three more plunks.

Glitters of yellow and red flickered like flames on the water and dotted the rocks all around. Blinking in astonishment, I focused again, but the colors were gone. I tried glancing sidelong at the pool. If I didn't look directly, I could just catch the sparkles.

A shadow fell over me, and I turned quickly to see Hazel.

"Did you hear something, Hazel?" I asked.

"Just water—why?"

"I thought I heard some kids playing," I said, trying to identify the sound accurately.

"Could be the day care up at Henderson's. They always have a passel of kids over there, and it's not far as the crow flies."

"Well, did you *see* something?" I pursued.

"I saw a reflection—a light of some sort," Hazel confirmed.

"So did I. I definitely saw some sparkles."

"I'll be switched," Hazel said in a puzzled tone.

"Maybe that's why they called this creek "Little Voodoo"—because of weird stuff like that," I suggested.

Hazel nodded. "Seems as long as I can remember folks been talking about oddball things happening here in these woods. Maybe because the trees are so old and huge. Gets the imagination racing."

"That's exactly what I think," I agreed.

Hazel gazed into the forest. "Why, a long time ago I thought—well, I don't know what I thought." Hazel's voice drifted to silence. Her wrinkled face looked older than ever, wrung out and sad. Something in our conversation had disturbed her, and we walked back to the house without speaking.

The steady whack of Vincent's ax grew loud as we neared the woodshed, and Hazel veered off to talk to him. I walked alone to the porch, pleased to find Ol' Cougar sprawled in the sun. Sitting down on the steps, I stroked the appreciative cat, who purred like a motor.

I thought of the flickering lights and those childish voices in the breeze. And I thought about my mirage girl and the disappearing dollhouse. "What's with these woods, anyway?" I asked Ol' Cougar, disturbing the quiet and halting his steady purr.

Glancing at the woodshed, I saw Vincent and Hazel examining a notebook together. Nodding and looking serious, Hazel gave Vincent a pat on the arm. "Keep it up," I heard her say.

Vincent returned the notebook to his jacket, and then left the way he had come, on the north-ward trail. Before he rounded the snowball bush, he turned and gave me a wave. "Later, Willa!" he called.

"Later," I said softly.

"So what's the deal with this Vincent guy?" I asked Hazel after lunch. "I mean, he seems like sort of a grouch." Hazel washed dishes while I dried.

"He's not so grouchy as he is unhappy," Hazel said. "He's had it rough since his mom died last summer. Ed can't seem to get over it."

"Who's Ed?"

"Vincent's dad. He's been hitting the bottle pretty hard since Rachel passed on. Manages to keep the muffler business going in Monroe, but their home life is awful slim. I don't think Vincent or Michael get an ounce of attention anymore."

"Who's Michael?"

"Vincent's older brother. Loves his motorbike—and cars. A tough guy, like his dad."

"I think Vincent is a tough guy, too."

"Oh, he's not so tough. Just trying to get along with his kin. He's an artist, like his mother. Darn good one, too."

"So Vincent's mother is Rachel Meeker, who painted the picture in the front room?"

"That's right."

"So Vincent lost his mom, and now his dad drinks too much?" It was the saddest thing I'd ever heard. I tried to get a handle on just how I felt about it.

"Some folks have a tough row to hoe, and that's the truth," Hazel said.

I remembered how Vincent had sulked in the kitchen. Maybe he thought I was moving in on his friendship with Hazel, the only person who gave him an ounce of attention anymore.

Poor Vincent. Not only did he lose his mother, he lost his father, too—at least the way his father used to be. Talk about change.

Everything had changed in our family, but Daddy was still the same guy. His letters were full of news and jokes and memories. He was trying his best with this bummer divorce; in my heart I knew this.

And Mama was full of energy and humor, thinking she could change the world, or Plunkit Used Books, anyway.

"Jeez, Hazel—I thought I had it so bad. I thought I had the worst row to hoe in history!" Tears welled up in my eyes and washed over the banks, but this time the pity I felt was not for myself.

CHAPTER 10

The Nutbones

LOOKING FORWARD TO STORY TIME, I got comfortable on the bed. Hazel sat in the rocker.
"Let's see, where were we?" Hazel asked.

"May had discovered the Nutfolk," I reminded her.

Hazel cleared her throat and began:

> May returned to the stump whenever she could escape her chores. She would not speak, or fidget about. She would only sit and watch.
>
> A family lived at the stump. May had seen them retire for the evening—

a father, a mother, three daughters, and a bent-over grandma.

May was amazed to see that the people could disappear and reappear at will, fading in and out of the atmosphere like vapor. They were a busy bunch, popping to places she knew not where, and later reappearing for suppers and such.

Other families lived at the high edge of the pond. They had built stick cabins and chinked them with mud and moss. All the windows were framed with pretty shutters, and all the doors were arched at the top and carved with what looked like family crests.

Stick cabins! I'd never mentioned my dream of the dollhouse to Hazel, and now she was describing the very image I recalled. A house made of sticks, decorated with painted shutters, hidden in the Voodoo Creek Woods. Coincidence? I didn't think so. What could it mean?

The stump house had the boldest crest—a cluster of acorns in front of two crossed bones. Over the acorns flew a carved banner with some Old English words on it. Below the acorns was the word NUTBONE.

May was intrigued by the Nutbone stump. Not only was it beautiful with its many balconies and bright green shutters, but it seemed to be the center of much activity. Little people came and went, children played, large meals were cooked on an outdoor stove, soap was made, and clothes were washed. There was a constant hubbub about the place.

Sometimes handsome boats would

sail the pond, or swim parties would meet at the beach in the heat of the day. May observed that it was usually the fathers who would appear to take charge of the children during these outdoor activities.

Fathers would fade in and out of thin air, often with babies on their backs in papoose fashion. They were fun-loving and patient; they weren't given to hollering at the kids. The tallest of them stood perhaps seven inches, while the babies were the size of peanuts.

The Nutfolk had in common a shade of golden brown to their skin, and a slight upward tilt to their eyes. Their clothes were well made and practical. Everyday garments were mostly pants and tops dyed either brown or green. Fancier clothes included fantastic embroidery and beadwork, often with a hint of American Indian in the styling.

At first, as May observed the little creatures, she thought of them as dolls come to life, as playthings for her amusement.

Dolls coming to life. Well, isn't *that* interesting. How could Hazel's fairy tale coincide with every crazy vision that I'd cooked up in my head? It was almost like she'd read my mind. It was almost like we'd read each other's minds.

. . . But as time went on May thought of them as people. As deep and complex as any person of any height.

One morning while May sat watching, she was horrified to see Bearboy, her family dog, galloping through the woods lickity-split to find her. Big paws apounding and long tail athrashing, he bounded toward her, about to squish Nutfolk Wood like a slobbering monster!

"No, Bearboy! Stop!" May ordered. But there was no stopping the dumb dog. Just before trampling the village, at the last possible moment, Bearboy jumped backward with a shocked yelp. He then inched forward, sniffed, and sat. His tongue lolled out in a comfortable pant, and he seemed content to wait.

The mother from the stump looked straight at May in surprise. She had been hanging clothes out to dry and seemed unconcerned about the dog. But May's attempt to protect the village attracted her full attention.

"Miss May Pocket, I presume," said

the lady in a droll tone. "So you can see us then?"

"Y-Yes, ma'am," May answered, startled at being spoken to and surprised that the lady knew her name.

"I'll be switched," the Nutfolk mama mumbled. She looked May up and down, apparently assessing the situation. Finally she said, "I am Momby Anna Nutbone. You may call me Momby Anna."

With her smooth brown skin and tilted eyes, May thought she looked quite beautiful. She was dressed in sensible work clothes, a tunic with matching trousers. She wasn't dressy 'cept for a bright red scarf wrapped around her head. And never mind her small stature. She managed to give off quite an air of command.

May felt shy in the presence of the

regal Momby Anna. "How do you know my name?" May asked.

"Well, May, we're neighbors, aren't we?" Momby Anna answered vaguely. "Besides, I've seen you about, but I was not sure that you were an enlightened human girl."

"What do you mean, 'enlightened'?"

"It's exceedingly rare for a human to perceive us. Here in Nutfolk Wood we use a mild magic to keep curious eyes from focusing. It takes a certain mind-set for a human to see through our screen."

"How is it that I can see you? I'm nothing special," May said modestly.

"On the contrary, Miss May. You must be special indeed. You must be a girl who lives in the moment, and you must love nature to boot. The black-haired folk who once inhabited these woods saw us frequently. Ah, but times have changed," Momby Anna sighed.

"How did you stop my dog?" May asked, perplexed at Bearboy's strange behavior.

"Basic senzall." Momby Anna thought for a moment how to explain. "It's like the stuff of lightning, only quite harmless. We always rig senzall around our dwellings and ourselves. Then if intruders—like your dog—pose a threat, the senzall gives a little kick. The harder and faster the oncoming forces, the more extreme the senzall. A slower approach would have encouraged a mild reaction, like an itch. Never fails to urge the intruder to take a different path without really knowing why," Momby Anna finished, looking amused.

She was less clear about the Nutfolk ability to disappear and travel from one place to the next. She said only that it had to do with small particles, and that Nutfolk called it "surging." She claimed it was a skill to be learned, like most things.

Using these age-old methods, the Nutfolk had kept themselves safe and undiscovered for generations. Momby Anna said that they had settled in this land long, long ago. They had traveled across oceans, escaping the tyranny of certain power-loving fairies.

Momby Anna looked serious when she said, "May, you must be ever so careful about who you tell. We Nutfolk have survived in this land by being discreet. Do you understand what I am saying?"

"Are you asking me not to tell

anyone about Nutfolk Wood?"

"I'm just asking you to be cautious about who you tell. Besides, many a human has been labeled crazed for claiming to see little people. You know this to be true."

Momby Anna was right. The Suquawkle Valley might have been rural, but it was far from the "old countries" where people were steeped in legend and superstition. Folks here were progressive, and logical thinkers.

Of all the fields and woods in all this great land, the Nutfolk had settled in May's backyard.

Not a human could see them, and not a human could know them but May Pocket.

Who could she tell?

No one.

CHAPTER 11

Plain and Simple

❦

"MAMA, DO YOU THINK there is such a thing as fairies?"

"No I don't, Sweet Pea, but it's a nice idea. Why?"

"Hazel's been telling me fairy tales about these little people who live in a stump, and this human girl who finds them. I wish stuff like that were true."

"You mean stuff like magic?"

"Yeah, like magic, or like undiscovered mysteries. It would be neat to solve a mystery or discover something new."

"Well, we don't know everything, do we, Wil?

I mean, people haven't solved every mystery."

It was Sunday evening, and Mama had fried up some hamburger patties and put frozen French fries on a cookie sheet to bake. She knew I liked that combo, plus it was quick. We sat down for dinner and Mama pretended not to watch every bite I took. "Eat your peas," she mentioned casually.

I told Mama all about Vincent Meeker, May Pocket, and Voodoo Creek, and Mama told me about the bookstore, and business, and her plans. She wanted to paint Plunkit Used Books, have new signs made, and advertise in the *Banner*. First she needed to make a deal with Herb Moss, the owner.

"What kind of a deal, Mama?"

"A good deal for a lazy man," Mama answered, but would say no more.

That night, staring at the puffy clouds in my little bedroom, I snuggled with Ratty-Monkey. There was a lot to think about. Before I could fix my thoughts on any one thing, I was asleep. And then a lemon sun peeped through my daisy curtains. It was Monday, wash day at Hazel's.

I had no idea that getting clothes clean could be so much work. We lugged the dirty clothes out to the wash shed and stuffed them into a barrel sitting sideways on a frame. This was Hazel's "washing machine." Next we heated the big pot of water on the stove, and poured the water into a funnel on a pipe, which channeled it down to the washing machine.

Then we went back out to the wash shed so Hazel could add detergent and put me on "churn" duty. There I sat, pumping the churn stick, which rotated the barrel by quarter turns. Water kept dribbling out the cracks, soaking me and getting my sleeves nice and clean. My arms were aching by the time Hazel said I could stop.

To my dismay, we had to drain the soapy water out of the washing machine, add clean water, and then slosh again to rinse. We put each article through the wringer to get the excess water out. Finally we hung it all up to dry. Hazel had two more loads to wash. This pioneer business was losing its charm.

When the last towel was hung, I proudly stood back and admired the clothesline, so organized, so fresh smelling. A thought occurred to me. "Hazel, what do you do in the winter?" I asked with dawning horror.

Hazel chuckled. "Usually I do the wash in the bathtub. I use that washboard hanging above the tub. And I try to keep my loads small. The wet stuff gets hung on the dryer rack set up next to the stove. Keeps the house *humidified*," she joked.

"I don't know how you do it. It is so much work!" Suddenly inspired, I said, "Hazel, maybe one of your children could come back here in the winter and help you with your chores."

Hazel's face took on a careworn expression as she replied, "My Henry died in the big war, so he's been gone all these many years. And my daughter Kathy—Katherine and I—well, we just can't seem to get on."

Hazel seemed like the easiest person in the world to get along with. "Why can't you get on with Katherine?" I asked.

"Well, sometimes children decide to be the opposite of what riles them about their parents. Jack and I were plain and simple folks, as you can see. But my Kathy wanted what was fine and fancy, and by gum, she got it. Married into money—'course money comes in handy, that's for sure. It's just that Kathy thought money was the end, not the means."

Hazel gazed out at the laundry line, quiet. I didn't want to bug her with more questions, even though I didn't understand what she was talking about. I reached for her hand to hold and said, "I like you plain and simple, Hazel."

For a few moments Hazel would not look my way. She sniffed, and wiped her eyes. "We deserve a treat," she finally said, and we walked hand in hand to the house.

The day was warm and I was sweaty from the heat and hard work. Inside the house it was cool and comfortable because the maple blocked the afternoon sun.

"I made us something special last night," Hazel said with an impish grin. "I think we'd better eat it up, then if we have room, we'll have lunch."

Hazel pulled a canister out of the cramped freezer box. She had made ice cream. It was creamy vanilla, as delicious as only homemade ice cream can be. She let me scoop out as much as I wanted, claiming she was trying to fatten me up.

After we pigged out on the ice cream, Hazel suggested we rest a spell on the porch.

"I'll fix us some iced tea and you can drag out that old quilt and take a load off—and get yourself a pillow."

First I ran to the line and whipped off a clean pillowcase so I could enjoy the fresh-smelling linen.
Then I arranged the quilt and pillow and lay back
on the porch floor, my arms behind my head.

It was pleasant on the porch, shaded by the
maple, perfumed by the honeysuckle. Now and
then a bee buzzed or a bird sang. The ice in our
glasses tinkled and snapped as we drank. Hazel
rocked contentedly in the old rocker. The creak of
the chair joined the chorus of birds, and bees, and
tinkling ice. It sounded like summer to me.

"Thanks for the help this morning, Willa. That
was a heap o' hard work," Hazel admitted.

Ol' Cougar joined us on the porch, but he didn't
want to snuggle because of the heat.

"You tired of that May Pocket stuff?" Hazel
asked.

"No way! In fact, I think you ought to write it
down, on account of it's so interesting. Did you
make up May Pocket yourself?"

"I did make it up, a long time ago," Hazel answered in a melancholy voice. "All right, all right—now where were we?" She sipped her iced tea and picked up the story:

As the weeks went by, May met the Nutbone children and discovered that, like human kids, they had distinct personalities, talents, and problems, too.

The oldest Nutbone was Rain. She was a beauty with dark hair and earthen eyes. May rarely saw her because, as Momby Anna explained, Rain was practically a grown woman and had her own life to lead. Rain surfaced occasionally for suppers and holidays, and she usually brought a boyfriend.

May could tell that Momby and Poppy didn't approve of the boyfriend.

They said things like "So, Ronald, how goes farming?" Or "Ronald, how be that baby cousin of yours?" These were subjects that a Nutfolk fella would normally enjoy discussing. But Ronald would blush and squirm, and he'd confess that his music was taking all his attention.

Ronald was a student of the harpolin, a Nutfolk stringed instrument. He played beautifully, but Poppy worried that a musician was not a good match for his Rain. Momby grumbled that no one was a good match for Rain—that Rain's aura was the steadiest and brightest that Nutfolk Wood had seen in years, second to none 'cept for Momby herself.

You see, each Nutfolk was known not only by voice and face, but by aura as well. The aura was a halo of

*light radiating from every Nutfolk.
Different shades in the aura repre-
sented different personality traits or
strengths. May could only detect auras
through the corner of her eye. When
she looked directly at a Nutfolk, the
aura vanished.*

As Hazel spoke, my brain seized the phrase about
detecting auras through the corner of the eye.
The auras seemed just like the sparkles I'd seen in
the woods—undetectable if I looked directly at
them.

"Hazel," I interrupted, "*I* saw sparkles. One
time down by the Gypsy Wagon and the other
time near the creek with you. Maybe I can see
auras like May!"

Hazel smiled. "Well, Miss Wil, the forest is full
of light and shadow—"

"I know! But we saw something sparkle—didn't
we?"

Hazel hesitated. "This is just a story," she finally said. "I'll tell you the rest."

Rain was special because her aura was strong and steady. She glowed like a leader. She glowed like her mother, who'd been head-woman of Nutfolk Wood for years. Momby Anna recognized Rain's potential, and hoped that Rain would someday be asked to lead, and then she (Momby) could retire from politics. But Rain hadn't shown much interest in community affairs. She was mostly interested in the harpolin-playing Ronald.

June was next oldest, a brown-haired pixie with green eyes. She always wore an acorn cap, despite reprimands from Momby about hygiene. She was first at the beach and loudest at a party, and was forever cooking up jokes, dances, and games.

June privately bemoaned her lack of a steady aura. It was embarrassing for a Nutbone to glow so feebly. Momby Anna scolded June for paying more attention to fun and games than to the Learning Circle—that's Nutfolk school—and Momby was right.

May had once complimented June on her beauty, saying, "I do think you're the prettiest girl I've ever seen, big or small."

June brushed the words aside, saying bitterly, "All the Nutbones are fair of face—not like it matters. Nutfolk don't pay much attention to faces—it's auras that count. There is a Nutfolk saying: 'Beauty glows from the soul.' And it just so happens that I'm not very blessed in that department. I guess I play the clown a lot because of my pitiful aura." June was embarrassed and downcast.

"June," May said, trying to be tactful, "there is a human saying that goes: 'Act the way you want to be, and soon you'll be the way you act.' I think you act so kind and friendly and full of fun—you'll get your aura someday."

June stared at May for a long moment, then thanked her with a formal Nutfolk thank-you, her little finger to her heart, followed by a solemn bow. May spied a tear in June's almond eyes, and she was deeply touched.

Plum was the youngest Nutbone. She was a blondie with gray eyes and round rosy cheeks. Plum was quiet, and glowed with the steady seriousness of her sister, Rain. It was Plum who

Poppy usually took farming because she always begged to go. She loved farming and had a knack for plant magic. Poppy sometimes worried that Plum might be too boyish in her interest in farming, but he was wise enough to know that a child's healthy interests should be encouraged—never mind the traditions of what a boy or girl ought *to do.*

Farming for Nutfolk meant helping out with a human garden, and then taking a percentage of the harvest. The Nutfolk eliminated weeds, kept out bugs and critters with senzall, and encouraged the plants to grow. It was a fair trade.

Plum was pretty good at the growth spells, but one afternoon she got carried away, creating some monstrous green beans.

Growth spells? This time I did not interrupt. But really, the coincidences were piling up. I could clearly envision that crazy trillium growing in fast motion and then shriveling into dust.

Hazel kept talking.

> *May found Plum in a panic under the beans, trying in vain to conjure them away, so May pulled them all up and buried them under the compost pile, swearing she'd never tell a soul.*
>
> *Once the enormous beans were buried, May and Plum fell into a fit of giggles over the predicament. They had a good laugh, but Plum said later that the Nutfolk were very careful about spells and alterations.*
>
> *"We live our lives in secret. It is the only way," Plum said gravely.*

There was a lengthy, silent pause. I glanced up to

see that Hazel had talked herself to sleep. An airplane buzzed long and low somewhere overhead.

I sniffed the freshly laundered pillowcase and wondered what the pretty embroidery stood for. Lazily I fingered the hem with the old-fashioned, curly stitches that spelled out H.M.W.

Before the airplane quit complaining, I too had dozed off.

In a dream that rolled by like a movie I saw the letters *H.M.W.* float off the linens on the clothesline and swirl over to the garden. The gray rabbit was there, munching busily, but he paused to say, "Hazel *M*. Wicket."

Then he asked, "Hazel *Marie* Wicket?" He puzzled over that for a moment and asked, "Hazel *Margaret* Wicket?" He munched while concentrating some more, and finally, looking triumphant, announced, "Hazel *May* Wicket!" He blinked at me, and I woke with a start.

Feeling groggy from sleep and heat, it took me

a moment to figure out where I was, and why. I was sideways on the quilt, on Hazel's front porch, and I had drooled all over my pillow. Staring at the pillow, I had a thought form sluggishly until it became an idea. The idea hit me like a slap in the face.

Hazel May Wicket and Miss May Pocket? These two girls had an awful lot in common. They lived in the woods in the olden days, they were nature lovers, and had similar names.

And the tone of the Nutfolk tales—the way that Hazel told them—sounded so convincing, so full of detail.

And what about these Voodoo Creek Woods where strange things kept happening? To old Indians, to pioneers, to hunters, and to me.

Everyone knows there is no such thing as fairies. But something in my gut told me that Hazel was not *everyone*.

CHAPTER 12

Hazel May

"I'M BUYING THE BOOKSTORE," Mama announced, looking smug and completely determined. "I'm going to make old Herb an offer, and he's too dumb to refuse."

I wanted to talk about Hazel May and the Nutfolk, but Mama wanted to gab about business. She was wound up like a spring over this deal, and I could see that I wouldn't get a word in edgewise.

The evening was warm, but the droning fans in the Gypsy Wagon kept us comfy. Mama talked about what the lawyer said, and what the banker said. She spoke of mortgages, profits, and losses.

I sat on the sofa and listened, and as day faded to dusk, Mama's words softened into dreams.

"Sorry I blabbed you to sleep last night," Mama said in the morning, apologizing. She'd carried a cup of mint tea into my bedroom and said with gusto, "Drink up! I've got a business to buy."

Despite Mama's enthusiasm, I had a twinge of fear. The last of our savings would be thrown at Plunkit Used Books. Though Mama called it "a diamond in the rough," I had a hard time seeing anything remotely jewel-like in that old building.

But I was sick of worrying. I was tired of worrying. I was actually bored by the thought and the feel of worry. I wished I could clean out my brain and sweep all that worry right out of my ears. I pretended to do it, too. I even leaned my head sideways so the worry could fall out. I thought of how nice it would be to get some fresh air into my brain, and maybe place a bouquet of flowers where the worry had been.

Some worry *did* leak out of my ears that morning, of that I was sure.

I sniffed. Tuesday was bake day for Hazel, and I could smell something good all the way down the road.

I decided to hold my tongue about Hazel May and the Nutfolk stories, at least until I could think of a way to approach Hazel.

"Better get yourself one of those cinnamon rolls before I eat 'em all up," Hazel warned.

I smirked because I'd learned that Hazel ate like a mouse and probably couldn't finish a roll if her life depended on it.

She sat me in front of a steaming, buttered cinnamon roll and a glass of milk, accompanied by a side of crispy bacon. I didn't even have time to think about a stomachache before I was done and full.

After breakfast, Hazel gave me a lesson in bread

baking. She kneaded her big pile of dough, and I kneaded a smaller version. I copied her roll-roll-squish-pump action and was enjoying bread baking. But I had questions burning in my mind, and the time had come to get some answers.

"My middle name is Jane—Willa Jane Mackenzie," I announced breezily. "Mama named me after authors she liked. I wish my middle name was Jo. I'd like to be Willa Jo—sounds more spunky." I figured I was being pretty clever sneaking up on the subject from this direction. I went on, "So what's *your* middle name, Hazel?"

Looking at me sidelong, Hazel kept kneading, then answered, "May—Hazel May."

Kneading my dough with exaggerated concentration, I paused thoughtfully, then said, "Hmm, that's sort of funny—how May Wicket sounds a lot like May Pocket. Don't you think that's sort of funny, Hazel?"

When Hazel just agreed, I continued the strategy.

"You know what else is funny? You were a little girl who lived in the woods just like May Pocket."

Hazel kneaded on, but now with a shadow of a smile.

"And the final thing that's funny is that when you were a girl the old Indians around here called this place Kloshe Tenas-Tillicum Chuck," I said dramatically, quoting the Plunkit history booklet. "Do you know what that means, Hazel?"

The kneading action stopped short. Startled, Hazel looked directly into my eyes and answered, "It means you are a little dickens, Miss Willa Jane. Yes, I know what that means. I know better than anyone."

"Happy Little-People Creek. That's what the Indians called this place in the old days." Hazel sat in an ancient metal lawn chair. I was sprawled at her feet on the quilt. We had brought our iced tea outside for a rest under the maple tree while the bread rose. Hazel had promised to explain a few things.

"In those days there was a lot of talk about odd things happening around Voodoo Creek, and the Indians hereabouts swore that these woods were enchanted. But I never saw nor heard anything strange, except for occasional sparkles in the underbrush. Yes, that's right. But I always explained them away with the likes of shiny leaves, or sun dapples, or discarded bottles.

"The summer I was nine—just about your age, Willa—I saw something strange indeed." Hazel looked pensive as she gathered memories from that long-ago childhood:

I was my parents' only child. I was happy enough, but I yearned for a sister so I'd have someone to play with. When Ma told me a baby was coming, I was thrilled. A baby wasn't exactly a playmate, but it would be someone to fuss over, and eventually she'd have to grow up. (I just assumed it would be a girl.)

The day that Ma told me about the baby, I saw the Nutfolk. I came across the stump just like I told you, only it wasn't May Pocket who made the discovery. It was nine-year-old Hazel May Cole.

At first I thought I'd lost my marbles, seeing those little people. I dragged my dad down to look at the "interesting stump," just to see what he might see. He liked the pretty glen, but it was obvious that I was the only one seeing fairies.

I was an isolated only child, way out in the country, and suddenly I found myself amid a fun-loving family and a bustling village. I quit worrying about my sanity and decided to enjoy myself.

As the weeks passed, my ma grew more and more tired. She looked awful pale, and moved like an old lady, weak and achy. By midsummer the doctor told her to take to her bed and stay there.

I cooked and fetched and cared for my ma. She explained that some ladies have a harder time than others, and I ought not to worry. She'd say, "Hazel May, you are one good little nurse, but even nurses need fresh air—now you scoot."

So I would scoot, and play in the woods like I'd always done. But in the back of my mind lurked a fear and a dread that I did not want to stir up. I knew that Ma was in trouble.

Was it squelched-down fear that prompted me to conjure up a world of *make-believe? Or was I so open for tidbits of happiness that I really saw the little people I'd heard tell of?*

By August my dad had arranged for a manager to take his place at the hardware store. Throughout that month he stayed home and worked around the house. He fixed the screen door and the front gate, and puttered about, but mostly he'd just sit with Ma. He would read articles to her, or write letters that she would dictate, or he'd rock quietly while she slept.

Dad bought a bell with a handle, and instructed Ma to ring it if she needed anything. Ma laughed and said she felt like Mrs. Vanderbilt ringing for service. The bell would be used only for emergencies.

With Dad doing some of the cooking and fetching for Ma, I was freed up to *wander, and wander I did. The weeks passed quickly with my new friends, the Nutfolk. The weather stayed fair all through August as I learned the wonders of a whole nother culture.*

The Nutbones were as kind as they could be, and sometimes they felt more real to me than my own family. But I don't think I knew what was real and what was not that summer. Until the bell rang.

Another gorgeous day had bloomed, and I was playing a rock game with Plum and June on the banks of Little Voodoo. June was winning, and doing a hoochie-koo dance to rub it in. I heard the bell and didn't realize at first what it meant. It tinkled through the woods before emergency *rose up in my brain. The Nutbone sisters disappeared instantly, as did their tiny footprints and the pebbles from our game.*

"Oh, Ma," I whispered. Then I yelled, "I'm coming, Ma!" though only the woods could hear me. I ran as fast as I could force my legs to go. I came out on the north trail and jumped the same fence that Vincent jumps. I was little but I soared over that fence like a thoroughbred. I hit the porch and slammed the screen door behind me when my dad yelled from Ma's room, "Don't come in here Hazel May!" My legs carried me there, anyway.

Having babies is messy business, but there was something wrong with Ma. The baby was early. There was too much blood. Dad said to go get Grandma Henderson, so I took off running again.

Grandma Henderson was the local midwife on the property one over from Meeker's, where they do the day care now. I rushed the old lady out the door, and we rode her swayback horse, Myrtle, back to my house.

We found Dad in the bedroom, tearful and silent, holding Ma's hand. He said, "May, your Ma is gone."

She hadn't made it. And neither had the baby.

We buried my ma and the baby down in Plunkit cemetery. After a summer of sunshine, it rained on their funeral day. Under my dad's black umbrella I said good-bye to Ma and my little sister. You know, I still miss them today.

"Now how can an old lady miss a baby sister she never really had?" Hazel asked.

"Oh, Hazel," I croaked unsteadily. I did not want to look at her for fear of breaking down. We sat quietly for a long while, thinking our thoughts.

Finally I dared to ask, "Was it true, Hazel? Did you see the Nutfolk?"

"To this day," Hazel replied, "I do not know the truth. I suspect I imagined it all to escape from worrying about my ma. But when I recall the details, they seem so real. How could I have thought up such a yarn? All I know is that the magic ended when the bell rang. I never saw the Nutfolk again except in my dreams. So many dreams."

The corners of Hazel's mouth turned down. She was done talking. After a long silence I ventured to ask one more question: "Hazel, is that why you never changed this place? You know—never brought in electricity and stuff?"

Hazel looked sheepish, sad, and tired all at once. "Nutfolk like things plain and simple," she said, "and so do I."

CHAPTER 13

Soul Sisters

S URE ENOUGH, "lazy Herb" sold Plunkit Used Books to Mama, lock, stock, and barrel. She and Vivian cleaned the bookstore like it was war waged with detergent. Then she hired the Fetch Brothers to come in and paint the walls and all the shelving, and the floor, too. The place looked rich in shades of brown, dark green, and tan.

Mama liked being the boss. She fired Gretchen, the book buyer, for being "a dingbat," and gave Vivian a raise. She had the front sign painted proper, so it no longer said PLUNKIT US BOO . Now it read PLUNKIT USED BOOKS, ESTABLISHED 1955.

With Mama's new role at the bookstore, I was spending more time at Hazel's. Our days were shaped by Hazel's old-fashioned schedule, utterly reliable and consistent. We cleaned on Saturday, walked on Sunday, washed on Monday, baked on Tuesday, and on Fridays we went to market.

Going to market meant warming up the Chevy to make the trek into Plunkit and the Wise Deal. Everyone in the Suquawkle Valley and the foothills did their big shopping at Wise Deal, where efficiency always came second to conversation.

While the car warmed up Hazel would check her shopping list, pin on her hat, collect her bulging black purse, and then recheck her list. We'd eventually shuffle out to the Chevy, which probably gulped about five gallons of gas during the twenty-minute warm-up. After eyeing all the knobs and dials, Hazel would finally wrestle the gearshift into drive, and we'd creep out of the carport.

Hazel definitely drove like an old lady. She gripped the steering wheel white-knuckled and tense, leaning forward in a hawklike posture. She wouldn't let me tune in the radio because she feared the distraction. Despite Hazel's nerves, I liked driving in the Chevy. It was wide and elegant, and I didn't have to buckle up because there were no seat belts.

Friday dawned balmy and fine as I walked alone to Hazel's house. Her shrubs and flowers were in wild competition to outbloom the next guy. There was a pie cooling on the porch rail, and Hazel was laying down the law to Ol' Cougar, who was looking offended.

"Now most felines would not be fond of apple pie, but Ol' Cougar likes my pastry," Hazel explained.

Ol' Cougar turned slowly, tail up to show his disdain for the pie, and the insinuation that he might be a sneak.

"Oh, don't go away mad." Hazel smirked at the cat. "Just go away."

"Do we need to make out the shopping list?" I asked, knowing the drill by now.

"I think we ought to have us some breakfast and then go for a walk." It was unlike Hazel to vary from the routine.

"Aren't we going shopping?" I asked, a little miffed at the change.

"We'll go this afternoon. I thought while it was cool I'd show you some of the places I played as a girl," Hazel said.

"Could you show me the Nutfolk stump?" I asked eagerly. I felt a growing sense of excitement, as if something would be revealed.

"I think it might be good for me to visit some old memories," Hazel said. "Maybe I kept too much to myself for too long. Guess now I've got a sidekick to share it with." Hazel cocked her head my way.

I smiled at Hazel, and took her hand, not much

bigger than my own. "You do have a sidekick, Hazel." I glanced back at Ol' Cougar and the pie. "That pie sure smells good," I said with my most sugary manners.

Hazel had coffee, and I had mint tea. We made a good dent in the pie, topping our slices with big scoops of ice cream.

After collecting her walking stick, we took to the trail behind the carport and made for the bridge. Walks with Hazel were always slow and steady.

"My Jack built this bridge," Hazel said proudly as we approached the handsome structure. "But when I was a little girl I just had to jump that creek."

"I can jump it, Hazel—watch me!" And I did, proof that I was growing better and stronger every day.

The trail zigzagged north. Hazel said it followed the old property line, and the other side of the trail was Ed Meeker's land. "Rachel Meeker and I walked this trail to visit each other."

"Were you and her best friends?" I asked.

"Now that you mention it, I guess she was my best friend, around here, anyway."

"How long was she sick?"

"Well, she was up and down for two years. I didn't think she would make it through that last winter—she was doing so poorly, in and out of the hospital all the time. When she was home, I'd visit. I'd read to her and tell her stories. Told her my Nutfolk tales, and she sure got a kick out of them."

"Did she think they were true?" I asked.

"She was a grown woman," Hazel reminded me. "I don't think she believed in fairies."

"But she liked the stories?"

"Yes, she did. Said she would love to paint them. Said the stories made her yearn for the forest. And darned if she didn't improve!"

"Then what did she do?"

"She headed for the woods with her sketchbook and her pencils and paints. She was out there purt near every day, happy as a lark."

"But she didn't stay all better?"

"No. And it was a sorry thing. She looked healthier than she'd looked in years. She walked and sketched every day. Then come the end of August, she took a nosedive. Ed got her to the hospital but in twenty-four hours she was gone."

"So Rachel painted *Nature's Magic* last summer when she improved from the cancer?" I was trying to clarify things in my mind.

"That's right. Brought that painting over to my house one evening, all wrapped up pretty. Said it was a gift for her 'soul sister.' I laughed and made some joke like, 'If we're sisters our parents must have waited forty years between babies.' Rachel had laughed, too."

Hazel and I walked in silence for a while, and I thought hard about Rachel Meeker and her temporary improvement. One more summer to paint like crazy. I thought about the term that Rachel had used—"soul sister."

"I know what she meant," I said solemnly, "about soul sisters. It's like there are magnets inside that draw two girls together. And right off you understand each other, and right off you like each other. You can be so different, in looks and age and everything. But there are those magnets."

Hazel looked at me with one eyebrow raised. "I 'spect you're right about that," she said.

"Oh, I know I'm right. I'm pretty smart—about some things."

"Oh, I know you are," Hazel agreed. We both grinned like a couple of idiots.

CHAPTER 14

Nature's Magic

"I THINK THIS IS IT!" Hazel motioned ahead, and we picked our way through the huckleberries trying to follow the imprint of an ancient trail that led to the glen. A moment later we walked into sunlight.

"Recognize it?" Hazel asked.

"It's just like the picture." I stepped lightly and whirled around, taking it all in. Then I stopped short.

The Nutbone stump sat in the middle of a natural clearing. I stood gazing at it, staring as hard as I could stare, trying to see the mystical house that Hazel had described. The arched door, the green shutters, the cunning balconies, the tiny people. I looked sideways and through my lashes, but to my huge disappointment, the stump remained just a stump.

"Maybe I have too much on my mind," I theorized, "and I'm not in the moment so I can't see the Nutfolk." This notion struck me as logical, but it was also frustrating. And since frustration was not *enlightened*, around and around I went with too much on my mind. I finally gave up trying to see things that weren't there.

"Hazel, I'm going to go sit on that stump," I announced.

"You can try, Willa."

I approached, avoiding the itchy ferns. The closer I got, the scratchier and more irritating the underbrush became. At the foot of the stump I thought surely I'd brushed by something poisonous because my arms and legs itched something awful, and my head began to ache.

"I don't feel so good. Is there poison ivy around

here?" I turned to ask.

To my surprise, Hazel was laughing herself silly over my misfortune. "Step away from the stump, Willa, and you'll feel better real fast."

Following my footprints back to Hazel, I found she was right. The headache vanished and the itching subsided.

"It's like Momby Anna said," Hazel insisted. "Something makes you want to turn away."

Other explanations lined up in my mind. "Maybe there's some kind of irritating spores in the air that come out when it's hot. Or maybe it's just that you told me about the itchiness, Hazel. Maybe my head is playing tricks on me."

"Maybe so. Maybe my head played tricks on *me* that summer." Hazel was quiet for a time. "I spent so many happy hours here. Look around. If this place isn't magic, I don't know what is. This here *is* Nature's Magic."

I had to agree with Hazel. A landscaper could plan and work for years to make a place look this beautiful, and here it was, by nature and by chance.

"When you were a girl and you saw this place, where was the village of stick cabins?" I asked.

"They were clustered over yonder to the left of the stump. There were maybe ten or twelve of them, built up on that incline. There was a town square to the front of the stump where all the little folks could gather, and a playground behind the stump for games."

"Hazel, do you remember any Nutfolk living around our Gypsy Wagon?" I had tried to come up with a plausible explanation for having pictured that stick cabin on our property before I'd heard the Nutfolk tales. But try as I would, nothing else made sense.

Hazel concentrated and recalled, "Old Gramby Nutbone kept a cabin there. She collected herbs for medicine, and worked healing spells. She was a cranky old thing, but she knew her stuff. Why? Did you see something down there?"

"I might have seen a cabin, but I might have dreamed it, too. Either way, it was definitely before I had even met you."

Hazel hunkered down on a nearby log to rest. She settled into story mode and told me of the old healer she had met so long ago.

I recall the day I saw a cabin there. I had wanted to talk to Gramby about good magic—I was thinking I could make my ma more comfortable. I checked the cabin by that weathered stump and found Gramby there sorting herbs.

"Excuse me, Gramby, can I ask you something?" I sat quietly for a long time waiting for Gramby to respond.

Finally she looked up and said, "I cannot help your ma, girl." Gramby was a sharp old tack, and she had me figured. "Your ma ain't enlightened, so Nutfolk magic ain't for her."

"Gramby, do you mean the magic will not work, or it's not allowed?"

"T'aint for her," was all she would say, and her voice was sympathetic, for Gramby, anyway.

I was making motions to leave, figuring our talk was over, when Rain Nutbone surged to Gramby's front door and immediately launched into a tirade.

"Gramby, I'll go crazy if I have to stay and lead Nutfolk Wood! Haggling over trade, arguing over harvest rights, officiating baby welcomes!" Rain moaned bitterly.

"I want to see something of the world, and I want to see it with Ronald. I must go, Gramby, or I'll never know peace, thinking about what might have been. We can trade off Ronald's music. He's traveled and he knows how it's done!"

Gramby sat, scowling. She always scowled so she was hard to read. Finally she said, "Listen, Miss Rain Storm Nutbone. Your Ronald don't know nothin'. And you don't know nothin'. But I 'spect it's time you find out how much you don't know—you better get yourself married and see the world."

Gramby's smile looked more like a snarl, but Rain hugged her and wept. "Thank you, Gramby. I love you," she whispered.

"Well, I know that," Gramby growled.

"And you, human girl. Don't you flap your tongue about this 'cause t'aint none o' your business."

"No, ma'am!" I answered, terrified

of the old lady.

Rain turned around, startled. She had been careless with her outburst in my presence. After noticing me, she slipped away, a little embarrassed, I think. I never saw her again.

The village was shocked to the gills at Rain's elopement because Nutfolk youngsters so rarely rebelled. They were normally a placid, sensible lot. Momby and Poppy were awful sad, but truth to tell, they were not so surprised. They had always known that Rain would be a leader. They were just sorry she had to leave home to do it.

Hazel was done with her story. The glen had been listening. Not a bird chirped, not a breeze whispered. Hazel closed her eyes. She was contemplating again.

I sat down next to Hazel, and leaned back

against the tree. The stump rose smooth and solid, like sculpture, from the roots. The pond lay at its base in shades of sky and evergreen. Moss and violets smothered the ground, and sunshine dappled down, painting the landscape in dabs of cool yellow.

I breathed the piney air. The hush lingered. Before my eyes the stump grew windows, green shutters, and a door. And to the left emerged the cabins, each claiming a different bright trim. Behind the stump were the game fields, and before it was the green, complete with gazebo for speeches and bands.

And there were the Nutfolk. They stood in small groups facing Hazel and me, as if they had been listening to the story and were waiting for more. Perhaps twenty small figures, just as Hazel had described them.

I turned excitedly toward Hazel, but she slept soundly, out for the count. Through my sideways glance I detected the sparkle and glitter of auras

from the crowd. I noticed one lady whisper something to another, and they all began to disperse,
returning to the business of the day.

In an upper-story window of the Nutbone
stump, a tiny face appeared, grinning mischie-
vously. It was the nutgirl in the acorn hat. She
winked and waved at me. I smiled, and stood to
move closer.

Suddenly it all disappeared. I woke up slumped
against the tree. A buzzing sensation moved sluggishly from my toes to my head, and my mind was
in a muddle trying to figure out what was real.

I gave Hazel a nudge with my elbow, and she
woke with a sputter.

"Hazel," I said, "I think I saw the Nutfolk! I
mean, I saw the whole village, and groups of
people, listening. They were listening to your
story I think."

Hazel's eyes blinked, and she looked first at the
stump and then at me. "Can you see them now?"
she asked hopefully.

"No. I only saw them for a minute, and I stood to move closer—but I guess I wasn't really standing. And then it all faded away." Doubt crept into my thinking as I realized I must have dozed off.

It was maddening. The image was like a dream. What was real and what was imagined were all mixed up in a blur of the glen and the curious tales of the Nutfolk.

CHAPTER 15

A Country Girl

"**H**EY. YOU WANT TO go fishing?" Vincent stood on the porch of the Gypsy Wagon with two fishing poles in hand. I was shocked to see him at my door, and felt like a goof in a nightie with puppies on it. It wasn't like we had gotten all that friendly up at Hazel's. We just small-talked because Vincent always had work to do.

"I've never fished before," I warned Vincent.

"Well it's no big deal. Mostly you just sit on your butt and wait."

"Okay. I'd like to go fishing. Let me ask Mama— she's sleeping in for once."

I rushed down the hall. "Can I go fishing with Vincent?"

"Go fishing with *who*?" Mama squinted at me from her rumpled bedsheets.

"You know—Vincent. That kid who helps Hazel out. He's got a pole for me and everything."

"Slow down, Willa. First you need to eat something."

"I had some cereal. I just gotta change. Okay, Mama?"

Mama smiled a little reluctantly. "Well, I guess you ought to have some fun once in a while. Go on."

Vincent and I were hiking down the driveway when Mama called us from the porch. "Come and get some lunch to take with!" She dangled a day pack, which I suspected contained the dreaded gingersnaps. "You kids have fun, and don't do anything stupid."

The morning promised heat, and smelled like hot pinecones and road dust. "So, where are we going?" I asked.

"There's a good pool down the road a ways. We'll give it a try."

I had some doubts about hanging out with Vincent. He was a boy, he was older than me, and he was so moody. But we had some things in common. We liked the outdoors. We liked animals. And we both liked Hazel.

For a while we took turns kicking a soda can. Vincent must have played soccer, because he started showing off how he could kick the can from his toe to his knee, and bat it from one knee to the other.

"That's pretty good," I said.

He whacked the can fiercely into the ditch. "We turn in here. Watch your step."

As we bushwhacked through the overgrown trail, I scolded myself for wearing shorts.

Finally we reached Little Voodoo, where the forest air was about ten degrees cooler. We trudged farther to a spot where two boulders squeezed the creek into a dark green pool.

"This is it," Vincent said. He scurried up the nearest boulder and found a comfortable ledge. "Come on up."

I scaled the boulder with no trouble, relieved that I could keep up and not seem like a wimp.

Vincent had brought worms in a container strapped to his belt. Baiting the hook was gross, as he wove the unlucky worm several times through with the hook. "You can't just poke it once or it'll fall off," Vincent explained.

We settled back to fish, and I eagerly watched my line, ready for action. After about ten minutes of scrutinizing pole and pool without a bite, I said, "So this is fishing, huh?"

"Yeah, this is fishing," Vincent said contentedly.

"I almost don't want to catch a fish because then I'll have to kill it," I added after several more minutes of quiet.

"My mom and I used to fish," Vincent offered

with no change of expression. "She liked to study and paint fish. She was a really good artist." Vincent paused. "I like to draw, too. And I still like to fish, even though . . . even though it always makes me think of my mom."

"You must miss her bad," I said, thinking of how I would feel if I lost Mama.

"Yeah." Vincent looked away. "Plus, my dad has turned into such a jerk. He can't hardly stand the sight of me without wanting to yell and complain about something. I guess I look too much like her and it weirds him out."

I looked at Vincent and said, "She must have been pretty." Then I realized the mushy compliment I'd just paid him. I stammered and started to giggle. "Not that you're pretty. I mean—actually you sort of have a nose like a wiener dog."

Vincent took the insult and returned one. "Well you're so scrawny I bet I could snap you like a twig."

"I'm stronger than I look! I've been doing laundry

up at Hazel's. See this muscle?" I closed my hand into a fist and pumped up my arm trying to produce a bulge.

Vincent's shoulders shook with laughter. "Oh there it is—I see the little nugget now!"

"Show me what you got," I challenged, remembering too late that he chopped wood every Sunday.

Proudly he showed off an impressive muscle.

"Okay, okay—pretty good—for a wiener dog," I conceded.

A tug on Vincent's pole and a flash of silver in the pool interrupted the flow of friendly put-downs.

"Dang! That fish was big," Vincent claimed. He reeled in his line and baited the hook again. "There's a big guy down there somewheres."

I peered into the dark pool, searching for the big guy. I felt a thrill of anticipation, and suddenly I knew I liked fishing. I scooted forward so I could better watch my line and scan the water. More time passed without bites or action.

I sighed, and dug through the day pack pulling out—what else?—gingersnaps. Mama had also thrown in a couple of apples, some peanut butter sandwiches, and apparently the only canned beverage she could find, tomato juice. "You want any of this?" I asked Vincent doubtfully.

"Yeah, I'm hungry."

I nudged the day pack his way.

After several minutes of listening to Vincent chew, I motioned toward the pool where the water flowed a marbly green. "I like that color of green."

"I like that color, too," Vincent agreed.

Birds twittered and the stream rushed noisily. We were in the shade keeping cool, watching our lines and awaiting the exhilarating tug from below.

"My dad is going to school in California," I said for conversation's sake. "He always wanted to go to college. He's going to be a computer programmer."

"Why'd your parents split up, anyway?" Vincent asked.

"They got married super young. I guess they sort of grew up and found out that they really bugged each other.

"They fight a lot?"

"I suppose so, but I was used to it."

"So is *your* dad being a jerk? I mean does he call you and stuff?"

"He calls. And he writes. Matter of fact, he writes constantly."

Daddy's last letter came two days ago.

> *Dear Willa,*
>
> *Your cousins are driving me crazy! Seems like all they want to do is watch TV and go to the mall, and they whine like babies if they have to walk a couple of blocks. I think Jackson and*

Lena have spoiled them. I know I'm being critical. I'm going to have to find my own place soon so I don't say something I'll regret.

It's funny. I thought all kids were like you—smart, eager, and tough. I didn't realize you were one in a million. Gosh, I miss you so much.

Take care, Willie,

Love, Daddy

I was deliriously smug over Daddy's letter. I read it again and again because it made me feel about ten feet tall. I guess the perfect cousins weren't so perfect after all. And maybe I was cooler than I thought.

Darn those spoiled cousins for bugging Daddy when he was working so hard. He was just trying to get training for a good job that he liked. Daddy was moving on with his life, but he would always be my dad, and I had a feeling that if he didn't see me soon it would hurt him maybe more than it was hurting me.

"I think he misses me a lot," I said to Vincent. "I miss him, too, but I have my rut."

"What do you mean, 'rut'?"

"Well, I know what to expect. It's the same thing every week up at Hazel's, and I like it that way. No surprises. No big changes. No divorces."

We glanced at each other. I suspected that the main thing Vincent Meeker and I had in common was the struggle to get over our sorrows.

"How did your parents get along?" I posed.

"They were pretty different, but they got along okay. I guess my mom liked how Dad knew everything about the woods, and he could fix things, too, and always find fun stuff to do. And for my dad, it was like Mom made him a better guy, with her books, and art, and thinking about God and stuff."

Vincent and I pondered the mysteries of our

parents for a while. Changing the subject, I asked, "Did Hazel ever tell you about her childhood? You know, growing up around here?"

"Not really. We usually talk about *me!*" Vincent laughed out loud as he realized that truth.

"I just wondered if she ever talked about some fairy stories she thought up, about these little people called Nutfolk who live in a big stump in a pretty glen?"

"No, but it sounds like a spot my mom used to paint. She must have done a hundred sketches of an old stump."

"Where are those sketches?" I asked, with a flutter of excitement.

"I don't know—packed away somewhere. My dad won't deal with any of her stuff. He got all mad about those drawings because he wanted her to be spending all her time with him." Vincent kicked his legs impatiently. "My dad had this grand plan to take her on the honeymoon they never had. Only thing was, she didn't want to go.

She wanted to stay in *her* rut."

"Didn't your dad want her to be happy, at home making art and stuff?"

"Who knows what he wanted, the selfish drunk." Vincent was glowering.

"I'd like to see those pictures," I said.

"What?" Vincent looked lost in sour memories.

"I'd like to see the sketches that your mom did of the stump."

"Well, like I said, I don't know where they are."

"Could you look around for them?"

"Maybe." Vincent wore a sullen mask. I was sorry the fishing trip was getting wrecked.

"Just because a person is a grown-up doesn't mean they're automatically smart. I mean, even grown-ups get, like, lost and messed up, and can't figure out how to fix things. That could be your dad, you know? Messed up and lost without your mom."

Vincent turned toward me and gave me a curious look. "You're a funny kid," he said. He grabbed a handful of gingersnaps. "I like these cookies," he added, crunching noisily.

"Man, we got skunked," Vincent complained. We hiked back up Wicket's road, fishless. The "big guy" had evaded us all day. Finally, hot and bored, we'd jumped into the creek, putting an end to any hope of a trophy. Cooled off and dripping, we walked leisurely home.

"Hey, Mama!" I called. She was cooking burgers out front on our rickety barbecue. "We got skunked!"

"Skunked, huh?" Mama looked at me smiling. "You're a sight, Willa."

I looked down at my damp self. Dust from the road had glued onto everything wet. Little rivulets of water still dripped from my hair, making paths through the dust on my skin. I was a mess.

"I'm a country girl now, Mama."

"No doubt," Mama said, and we cracked up.

Mama invited Vincent to stay for supper and he ate three hamburgers. I called him an oinker, and he agreed. He helped Mama clear the picnic table, and I know he got brownie points for that.

For the first time in a long time I felt like a happy, normal kid again. The sun went down, and Vincent went home.

I *was* a country girl.

CHAPTER 16

The Experiment

VINCENT WOULD BECOME my assistant and guinea pig, only he wouldn't know it. I devised a plan to put the Nutfolk Glen to the test and check out a theory I had. I just *had* to get proof positive or negative on that stump. Only trouble was I had never called a boy before.

The butterflies in my stomach were doing a rumba, and all the fluid had been sucked out of my mouth. Jeez! Get a hold of yourself, Willa. Vincent is just a *guy*—no big deal. But I feared his father might answer the phone and bark at me. Or maybe his brother would answer and tease me. Or Vincent might think I was a doofus to call since I was only a fourth-grader.

I checked under Meeker in the phone book and dialed.

"Hello?" It was Vincent.

"Oh, uh—hi, Vincent. This is Willa."

"Hi. What's up?"

His voice was encouraging. "Well, I was hoping you could check something out with me. I mean, there's this spot in Hazel's woods, and I think there's—well, I think there's something buried there."

"Like a body?"

"No, more like a treasure."

"So you want to go dig for a buried treasure?" Vincent made it sound pretty silly.

"Well, yeah. See, I think there is something buried behind this stump, and I want you to help me dig."

I couldn't stop dwelling on the glen and the Nutfolk stump. If Rachel Meeker had indeed drawn a "hundred sketches," maybe she had seen something. Maybe physical evidence was hidden "behind Nature's Magic."

"So, do you want to help me?" I asked, growing a tad defensive.

"Sure. When and where?"

"Meet me at Hazel's this morning. I don't have any chores until after lunch."

"Okay."

"Okay!" I hung up. That wasn't so bad.

Hazel agreed to our goofing off for the morning. She was clanking around in the kitchen as usual, while I waited impatiently for Vincent.

The day was heating up but Hazel's house was cool and clean. She'd put a cheerful vase of daisies on the desk under Rachel Meeker's painting. I studied the painting closely. BEHIND NATURE'S MAGIC, was carefully printed in the margin. *Rachel Meeker* was signed big and bold to the right of the title. The view of the stump was from the log where Hazel and I sat that first day we visited the glen.

Why had Rachel been so obsessed with that old stump? The glen was a beautiful spot, no doubt about that. But why focus on the stump? Artistically speaking, I suppose the stump was interesting. Was it "Nature's Magic"? If the stump was "Nature's Magic" like the title said, then what *was* the magic, and what was *behind* it?

Rachel could have meant the title to be like advice, reminding the viewer to look for natural beauty. Or maybe she meant it philosophically. Behind nature's magic is . . . what? Reality?

My thoughts chased around like a whirlpool. I wanted to believe that Rachel Meeker had seen something more, just as Hazel had so many years ago.

Vincent and I stood silent, spellbound by the Nutfolk Glen. Finally he said, "I've seen this place tons of times in my mom's artwork, only I never saw it in person."

"So you're sure this is the stump in all those sketches?" I asked. (Phase One of my experiment: stump identification.)

"This is it all right," Vincent whispered. He seemed entranced by the beautiful glen.

"Does that stump look at all strange to you?" (Phase Two: another witness to confirm a visual on the stump.) "I mean, do you see anything unusual?"

"All that's unusual is this place is so pretty. Why?"

"Just because. We gotta go around behind the stump. I'll follow you."

I stepped cautiously behind Vincent (Phase Three: reaction of another subject to the area), and noted with satisfaction that he veered as far *away* from the stump as he could, walking in a wide arc to get to the back instead of cutting the obvious straight line. Absently he began scratching at his legs and arms, then stopped abruptly. I quickly caught up to him.

"Is this a joke, Willa? Did you lead me into nettles?" he asked angrily.

"No way! There are no nettles here. Keep going," I urged.

After two more steps, Vincent put a hand to his forehead. Rubbing his eyes he said, "I don't feel so good. I think I'm allergic to something around here." (Phase Four: Does *un*informed subject grow itchy or ill?)

I decided to quit torturing Vincent. "Okay. Come away from the stump and you'll feel better."

We backtracked and sat on the log.

I told him everything. Starting with Hazel's long-ago summer, Voodoo Creek and my findings at the bookstore, and all of my dreams and mirages, including the village of Nutfolk Wood.

Vincent looked hugely skeptical. "Are you telling me that Hazel Wicket, the most sensible person in the world, believes there are fairies in these woods?"

"Well, that's just it! She *is* so sensible, like you say. But I've seen weird things, too! Like the sparkles, and the little doll-girl, and the stick cabin, and the dream in the glen. I know it sounds goofy, and maybe it is. That's why I need proof. Proof positive or proof negative. Like scientists get."

"Or like detectives?" Vincent asked mockingly. "We could run around the woods with big magnifying glasses looking for teeny-tiny people."

"You can laugh, but you definitely felt the itch, didn't you? And your mom spent a lot of time here, didn't she? In fact, she painted a painting that she titled *Behind Nature's Magic*, right? So what *is* behind that stump? Maybe *evidence*. That's what we need to find out."

"Okay, okay. But we got to dig in shifts or something because I swear that stump makes me sick."

Vincent and I suffered through the morning, digging and itching. When our heads began to throb, we'd switch off. If Hazel's description and my dream of the layout were correct, our digging would only rumple up the game fields, and nothing else.

In the end, we had dug an arch-shaped trench behind the stump, but came up with diddly-squat. Disappointed, I stood scowling and silent. Vincent was good enough not to snicker at me.

Carefully we filled in the ditch and patted the mossy turf back into place.

"If it makes you feel any better, I'll snoop around for those pictures," Vincent offered.

"Thanks." I felt like such a spaz. "I guess I got a little carried away. I thought for sure I was on to something," I said sheepishly.

"Well, maybe you are. Maybe we just got skunked."

I laughed. "Yeah, we got skunked."

"Anyway, I'm glad you showed me this spot,"

Vincent added. He looked around at the serene and pretty glen. "I can see why my mom was so happy here. I'm happy here, too. So long as I'm not digging."

CHAPTER 17

The Garden at Night

❧

"BORING ERRANDS AND LEGAL paperwork." That's how Mama described her upcoming trip to the city, topped off with the obligatory dinner with Grandma Cookie.

I rolled my eyes and groaned. "That sounds about as fun as a trip to the dentist."

Grinning, Mama said, "Don't worry. I didn't plan on torturing you in the first place. Thought maybe you could stay the night at Hazel's, then I'll pick you up regular time on Saturday."

I enthusiastically agreed.

Friday evening at Hazel's was *h-o-t*, hot. We ate

tuna salad and watermelon for dinner, then sat on the porch hoping for breezes. Hazel didn't feel like storytelling and I didn't feel like listening. The shadows grew long. Hazel worked a crossword puzzle and I read *Island of the Blue Dolphins*. Dusk settled before we knew it.

"Think I'll turn in," Hazel announced, yawning. "Can't seem to keep my eyes open past nine."

Oh, brother, I thought. A sleepover with an old person isn't exactly a party.

Hazel and I prepared for bed with toothbrushing at the sink and separate trips to the outhouse. I walked the long walk to the outhouse with a flashlight, checking all the nooks and crannies and stirring the toilet hole wildly with the spider stick.

Returning, I washed up at the kitchen sink with well water in a bucket, then changed into my summer nightie. I followed the golden glow of a kerosene lamp to Hazel's room and stood in the doorway.

The picture was like something out of the olden days, with Hazel's long white hair sprawled across a bleached pillowcase. Her nightgown was white, with fancy tatting at the throat. She held a paper-back novel in one hand, reading through granny glasses perched on her nose. The room glowed with the gentle warmth of kerosene.

"You look pretty, Hazel," I said impulsively.

I didn't mean pretty like a young girl, I meant pretty like a painting. Like maybe how Vincent would see her.

Hazel looked surprised and pleased. "Nothing like the dim light of kerosene to smooth out the wrinkles." She smiled and added, "If I snore, pinch me."

"Do you snore?" I asked.

"I'm not sure. Do you?"

"I don't think so."

"Guess we'll find out," she said good-naturedly.

Crawling under the sheet, I stayed well to my side of the bed as Hazel turned down the wick.

"Good night," we said in unison.

The windows gaped open, wide as they could go, with fitted screens to keep out bugs. Shadows decorated the walls, sharpened by a fat moon that had climbed up over the trees. With the sultry summer air, and no fan to lull me, I was quite sure that I would *never* get to sleep.

Irritation roused me to consciousness. I realized that Hazel was breathing a low and steady snorkel next to me. Nudging her did not affect the rhythm, so I took her at her word and pinched her. Her body jolted like she'd just received electric shock, and then she turned over, saying, "The gravy is burning."

I giggled quietly.

The pinch did the trick and stopped Hazel from snoring, but now *I* was wide awake and way too hot. After tossing and turning for many lonely minutes, I finally got up, determined to find someplace cool.

At the desk I wrote a note: "Hazel, I'm too hot and went to sleep outside, Willa." Then I placed the note on Hazel's bedside table. Wrapping the old quilt around me, I grabbed a sofa pillow and waddled out the door with the quilt dragging behind like a bridal train.

I'd intended to flake out on the porch, but it wasn't catching any breeze, plus it smelled like dust and cat hair. I wandered around the yard until it hit me—the garden bench!

With a lightbulb moon overhead, I could see real well. Closing the garden gate behind me, I shuffled down a bean row, which ended at the bench. The seat looked weird in the moonlight with its writhing sticks and strange formations, but the thing was surprisingly comfortable. Still curled up in the quilt, I reclined with my head on the pillow.

The night air felt mild and fresh. Leaves rustled occasionally with tired-out breezes. I felt safe behind the garden fence and snug in my quilt.

Yes, coming out here was a good idea.

My eyes blinked and drooped as I gazed at shadowy plants lit by that big yellow moon.

Low, singing voices preceded a parade of bobbing orbs. The voices sang a chorus that went . . .

> *Working owl shift ain't so bad,*
> *When you're working a pie moon night,*
> *And when your crew is strong and game,*
> *You'll be home by morning's light.*
> *That's right!*
> *You'll be home by morning's light.*

With bleary, doubtful eyes I watched a trudging gang of seven or eight Nutfolk-sized men toting what looked to be light globes hanging from fishing poles. They gathered near my bench, discussing some kind of work schedule.

A supervisor guy instructed, "Gents, don't bother with even a finger o' growth. These here veggies are perfect. Could maybe stand a touch of preservative, though. So just spread out and look for critters, and surge any weeds you find. Then refer to your harvest lists. All right, then . . ."

I sat up on my elbow, startling the group of men. "Are you real?" I asked.

The supervisor regained composure first, and slyly said, "Having quite a dream, aren't ya, girlie?"

"I'm not sure," I responded frankly.

"Of course you're dreamin'. Either that or maybe the old gourd has gone to rattles, eh?" All the men chuckled at this. I suspected they were referring to my sanity, and felt insulted.

"I think you are a farming crew from Nutfolk Wood," I said firmly, hoping to display what knowledge I could of the Nutfolk. "And you're out here to tend Hazel Wicket's garden."

This time Mr. Supervisor could not hide his

surprise. He whispered something to a crewman, and then he said, "You're a lucky miss to be in this here garden on a balmy full-moon night. Enjoy your dream, little girl."

From that point on, the crew ignored me, as if I'd never spoken—as if I were not there. They spread out into the garden and took to their task.

A voice shouted, "Hey, Jake! Gotta gopher mound in the corn—senzall the tunnel and spot for leaks."

"We got glow by the bench. Stead, take care of it."

At the foot of my "bed" a golden gas oozed from a hole in the ground. I watched from the folds of my quilt as crewman Stead dropped his globe down the hole, then called out, "Branch tunnel is senzalled and secure."

"We got gopher—midway to the corn!" another man yelled.

Amazed, I watched as a gopher scurried past, aiming for the tunnel by the bench. Almost to his hole—just as the animal's nose hit the glow of senzall, he froze, and squeaked once. Three small men surrounded the gopher and pointed the handles of their fishing poles at his body. Some unseen force lifted the stunned animal barely off the ground.

"Good catch!" the supervisor commended. "Stead, you and Jake and Winter get the old boy outside and senzall the perimeter."

Stead and Jake and Winter steered the hovering gopher with their fishing poles, nudging him up the bean row and out of sight.

"The rest o' you check your harvest list and get surging," ordered the supervisor.

A crewman thrust his pole into the ground next to the beans, illuminating the plants nicely. He touched a low-hanging bean at the stem, and it disappeared with a momentary humming sound. He proceeded to touch ten more beans, and they all hummed and vanished.

After referring to a small booklet, he grabbed

his pole and hiked into the cucumbers.

A man hollered, "Weed surged!" And another: "Slug on the lettuce!" A round of laughter, then: "Will ya look at 'em go! Just needed motivation." More laughter.

Straining to stay alert, I became aware of a gentle buzz, like a cicada. It was part sound and part feeling, and it seemed to be growing more intense. For some reason the buzz filled me with fatigue, luring me down into delicious sleep.

Drifting off, I heard a last round of the work song: "You'll be home by morning's light. That's right! You'll be home by morning's light."

I awoke to the sound of heavy machinery.

Swimming up, up from sleep, I remembered that I'd sacked out in the garden. On top of my quilt was Hazel's afghan; she must have come looking, and bundled me up.

What a strange and wonderful dream! With Nutfolk men and their work song, and a gopher roundup! Talk about weird.

The air had turned cool and misty, but my quilt cocoon was so cozy that I didn't want to get up. Somewhere an engine growled, and my stomach answered with a growl of its own. Finally I wriggled up and left the garden in search of Hazel and breakfast.

CHAPTER 18

Trouble and Worry

THE FRONT SCREEN DOOR was flung open. Unusual for Hazel, who was always so tidy and careful.

"Hazel!" I called cheerfully.

The house sat silent.

A thought dropped into my gut like a stone. Hazel was a very old woman. It was possible she had had an accident. It was possible she'd—I took the thought no further, but dropped the quilt and squeezed into my sneakers by the door. I raced around the house checking rooms, then jogged outside to the privy and the well house.

"Hazel!" I yelled again.

The only answer was the scrape and clatter of the heavy machinery, which was louder than before. I followed the sound.

"Hazel! Are you all right?" I called as I ran along the north trail, dodging branches and jumping roots. The turnoff path was just ahead.

Dread and confusion squeezed my stomach as I saw the deep tracks of a bulldozer where the slender trail to the glen should be. The dozer had come from the Meekers' side, busting down the wire fence and leveling the thick salal.

The rotting logs, giant ferns, and tall huckleberries were all gone, scraped clean away by the bulldozer that now sat growling at the edge of the glen.

And there was Hazel. Through the misty forest I saw her standing, all in white, her snowy hair loose and fluttering in a lazy breeze. She was still in her long cotton nightgown with soiled slippers on her feet.

"Hazel!" I shouted. She couldn't hear me over

the grumbling of the dozer.

Waving her walking stick in the air, she shouted at the driver. I moved closer to make out her words. "Ed Meeker, shame on you! This isn't your property!"

A red-faced and reeling Ed yelled back, "Y'old witch! I'm plowing this spot under. This spot ain't right. Some people spend way too much time here and it ain't right!"

Ed was drunk, and almost incoherent. He was struggling with shifting gears.

Hazel desperately whacked the dozer with her walking stick, trying to get Ed's bleary attention. "Edward Meeker! Rachel loved this place! How could you destroy something she loved so?"

"She came down here every shingle day!" he slurred. "An' Why? She was lookin' for fairies, thas why! 'Cause you filled her head with a bunch of hooey. She should-a been home with her family—with me!" Ed looked miserable and sick.

"And now my boy is asking questions. Wants to

paw through all her stuff and dig up the worst summer of my life." Tears filled Ed's eyes.

"Stop it, Ed!" Hazel snapped like a schoolmarm. "I'll have to get the sheriff," she threatened, though Ed could likely demolish the entire glen before help could even be called.

Hazel moved to the front of the bulldozer and whacked the blade with her stick. The sound of its impact was lost amid the rumble of the engine. "Now, Ed, you need to sober up. Turn this machine off and go home!"

"Move, ya crazy witch!" Ed yelled. "I'm headin' through!" He swayed wildly, trying to maintain his balance on the seat.

"Over my dead body, Ed Meeker!" Hazel stood tiny and resolute before the big dozer, her stick raised in defiance. Her white hair shifted in a whisper of a breeze. A shaft of sun penetrated the mist, causing a strange, glowing light throughout the glen. Hazel's hair and nightgown radiated a blurry halo. She looked frail and unearthly, like she could float away.

I stumbled forward, tripping on a tangle of branches. Ed saw me go down and threw me a scowl. Scrambling for footing, I kept checking to be sure that Ed hadn't found the right gear yet.

Suddenly Ed started flailing his arms and batting his head and body. He was acting like a man possessed. The dozer engine died as Ed grabbed the key and threw himself off the seat. In the heavy silence that followed I could hear his cries of pain. "Ouch! Dang bees!"

A swarm of angry bees had surrounded Ed. He was writhing and smacking himself furiously as he staggered up the trail. He disappeared, still swearing at his tormentors. "Ouch! Goll-danged bees!"

The sight would have been laughable had I not been so worried about Hazel. She leaned unsteadily against the dozer blade, apparently unharmed. The bulldozer had widened the turnoff path into a road, but the glen itself remained untouched. Hazel had stopped him, and just in the nick of time.

"Hazel, take my arm," I said. "Let's go home."

Hazel sorted out what happened while I put the teakettle on.

"I went out first thing and found you in the garden," she acknowledged. "That's when I put the afghan over you. I kept thinking something wasn't right when it dawned on me! The engine noise I was hearing was way too close.

"I didn't bother to change because I had a hunch there was trouble. I hurried up the trail, and there was Ed Meeker, *drunk as a skunk*, trying to operate his dozer. Guess in his mind he was burying that sad summer," Hazel said, shaking her head over Ed's pathetic behavior.

"It was strange how the bees came out of nowhere and started attacking Ed," I said, speculating. "Come to think of it, Hazel, the bees didn't hurt you at all, and you were right there—they just went after Mr. Meeker—chased him all the way up the trail."

"They didn't so much as land on me," Hazel agreed.

"Maybe the Nutfolk sent the bees," I said, hushed and dramatic.

"We don't know if there's any such thing," Hazel argued.

"I think the evidence is stacking up. I mean it was pretty weird—*coincidental*—that the bees attacked right at that moment."

Hazel looked pale and confused. "I just don't know. Maybe I am some kind of kook, hanging on to these fairy tales all these years. Maybe I got Rachel going on some squirrelly quest and she frittered away her last days." Hazel's hands covered her face. "I couldn't bear it," she said in a whispered cry.

It wasn't like Hazel to doubt herself.

"Why don't you go lie down," I suggested. "I'll get my own breakfast and start the chores. And don't worry about that crazy Mr. Meeker."

An expert worrier, I knew it was pointless to tell Hazel not to worry, but somehow it made me feel better. I figured Hazel was just upset by the bizarre morning. I figured she just needed to rest and get her bearings. Well, I figured wrong.

CHAPTER 19

Feeling Poorly

HAZEL GOT WORSE. She fretted over Rachel Meeker, the Nutfolk summer, and all the years in between. She doubted her usefulness and her sanity. Hazel was in what she would have called a "funk." And she did not seem inclined to pull herself out.

I was taking care of Hazel instead of the other way around, and I didn't much like it.

"I'm just feeling poorly," Hazel sighed. It was Tuesday morning, and she was still in bed and in her nightgown. Mama and I agreed that I ought to keep an eye on Hazel, but that if she did not improve, other arrangements would be made.

I'd meant to tell Hazel about my dream in the garden, but she'd been so wrapped up in her aches and pains she didn't seem interested in what I had to say. The mood was depressing at the homestead with Hazel acting so down. It made me think about something I didn't want to think about: Hazel was *o-l-d*, old, and she would not live forever.

The day was overcast and gray. I figured I'd get out of the house and do some gardening. With weeding in mind, I found gloves and a hoe in the carport. At the gate I surveyed the garden.

The zucchinis were gigantic. Fat radishes swelled out of the ground. The lettuce patch was a jungle, and the squash vines threatened to bust down the fence. The garden had gone completely crazy. Oddly, I couldn't find a single weed. On hands and knees I crawled through the paths. I peeked between radishes and lifted the skirts of lettuce. Nothing.

"These here veggies are perfect," the supervisor had said in my dream. I thought over the explanation of Nutfolk farming. The fairies took some of the harvest in return for tending the human garden. They eliminated weeds, kept out bugs and critters, and *encouraged* the plants to grow.

The little men in my dream seemed to be attending to all those tasks, but the thing was that it *felt* like a dream. A hazy, *un*real memory, patched together with Nutfolk stories and my own imagination. Could it have been something more?

The kid in me yearned for the magic, but the scientist in me demanded proof positive.

Since there was nothing to weed I returned to the house. "What do you want for lunch?" I called to Hazel from the kitchen.

When she didn't answer my heart beat faster, and I hurried to the bedroom in dread. The lump of covers on the bed lay still. I stared at the quilt until I saw it rise and flutter with

Hazel's measured breathing.

"Hazel!" I snapped. "What do you want for lunch?"

"What time is it?" she mumbled.

"It's lunchtime," I answered impatiently. A long pause settled, which I broke with a stern "I don't like this, Hazel."

"What don't you like?" Hazel muttered from under the sheets.

"This! You! I don't like you deciding you're all old and sick and gonna lie around like a blob!"

"I am old and sick, honey."

"Only because you're feeling sorry for yourself. So you're just going to give up."

"Well, I can't live forever."

"Then I don't want you for a friend!" I shouted. "I can't stand another big mess-up!" I had Hazel's full attention now. I gulped to explain.

"I thought you were strong. I thought I was your sidekick." Unwanted tears welled up and I swiped them away.

"I'm just a kid!" I cried, my voice high and quivery. "I don't *want* all these changes! I don't want people getting divorced and dying and everything. I thought I was safe at your house. I thought you could protect me from things, but you can't protect a flea!" I was weeping, and wondering all the while what the heck I was saying.

Hazel sat up in bed and stared at me with her mouth open. I turned and ran out of the house with a violent bang of the screen door.

Outside, I could hear the growl of a tornado. My stomach tightened into a crampy knot. It seemed like the tornado was everything bad, and everything bad was coming my way. I squeezed my eyes shut and put my fingers in my ears, shutting out the gloomy sound.

Jeez, Willa. Pull yourself together. So you had a little fit. You don't have to get all crazy over it. So some rotten things happen in life—you can deal with it. It's not a real tornado. There are no tornadoes here.

I opened my eyes and saw the dull overcast had given way to a misty drizzle. A familiar sound rumbled in the distance, but this was no cyclone. It was an engine. Oh no, not again.

I jogged the north trail and the rumble grew into an insistent whine. The noise rose with the rev of a throttle, accompanied by the pungent smell of gasoline and exhaust.

I turned onto the newly carved road to the Nutfolk Glen. The engine noise was screaming when I came face-to-face with a kid on a motorcycle. He looked like a young Ed Meeker. I figured he was Vincent's brother, Michael. He'd followed his father's drunken track to the Nutfolk Glen and now he was cutting figure eights into the violets.

"You're trespassing!" I screamed over the engine.

"Get lost," Michael sneered. He gunned his throttle and jerked forward, spattering mud on my chest as he fishtailed back up the bulldozed road.

"You're trespassing!" I screamed again. My heart thumped hard from fear and rage. Looking around, I gasped in horror at the ugly ruts he'd carved into the glen. I could have wept for the mess he'd made with his cruel tires and mindless speed. "Don't you care about anything?" I shouted, unheard.

The sickening whine of the dirt bike grew loud as Michael returned for more.

"There are no Nutfolk here," I whispered bitterly. Nothing stopped Ed's bulldozer, and nothing stopped Michael. I suddenly realized how much I had wanted to believe in Hazel's fairy tale.

Nutfolk or no Nutfolk, Michael Meeker would not destroy this glen with his stinking dirt bike. Over my dead body.

Unthinking, I jumped into Michael's path, arms forward, as if I had the strength to halt the big machine. I stood my ground, more angry than rational. "Stop!" I shouted at the lunging bike.

CHAPTER 20

Dreaming of Proof

I OPENED MY EYES to see a crowd around me—a very tiny crowd. They were as Hazel had said and as I had seen—the golden brown complexion with the tilted, almond eyes.

One of the little people stepped forward. "Brave Willa Jane," she said in a soothing lilt, "welcome to Nutfolk Wood."

I squinted and focused, trying to see around a rolling blur. "How do you know my name?" I asked.

"We've been watching you. We liked your aura from the first peek in your dream. And you glow so pleasantly in the forest. My name is Gramby Rain, and I am the healer here." She was an elderly Nutfolk with feathery wrinkles crosshatching her friendly face.

All around the periphery of my sight I saw dabs of light and color. It must have been the auras flickering from the crowd. It had not occurred to me that we humans might have auras, too.

"Now I best look at that arm." Gramby Rain was businesslike. "You have a nasty break, but we'll fix you right up. Lucky for you to be a tad enlightened because you'll take the healing. Don't you gawk at that arm now," she clucked. "Might make you a bit queasy. You just lie still while Gramby puts her hands on the problem."

I did as Gramby Rain instructed and did not move from where I'd fallen.

"So you can fix my arm?" I asked.

"Sure, and in a flash," she answered sweetly.

"So you can heal sick humans?"

"Only *some*," Gramby clarified.

Hesitantly I asked, "Did you try to heal Rachel Meeker?"

Gramby's face fell, and she answered sadly, "It was too late. We all liked Rachel, but the illness was advanced. I was able to help her through the summer, but she was simply too far gone," she sighed.

"Are you Rain Nutbone all grown up?" I wondered.

"Grown up and grown old." She smiled. "Long ago I met your friend Hazel, when we were very young. That was the summer I went north. And after all my travels, I came back to Nutfolk Wood as healer, and here I have stayed."

"Did Plum and June stay here, too?" I inquired.

"My sister Plum left when she married. She manages a large farm on the east side—very abundant. But June is here of course. She's head woman these many years." Gramby Rain turned to someone in the crowd and said, "Gramby June, come talk with Willa so she'll not fuss about her arm."

A noble-looking lady stepped forward. "Greetings, Willa Jane. I am Gramby June Nutbone. You met my daughter's daughter, I believe, the day that naughty girl surged to Hazel's and caught you in a dream."

"Yes! She wore an acorn hat. She told me that change is hard until change becomes the day. I didn't know what she meant, but I think I do now. All change becomes familiar, right? I mean, the sun has to come out eventually." My mind was wandering and I hurried back to the subject. "She was a nice girl, your grand-daughter, that is. She told me to be happy."

"A good-hearted lass," Gramby agreed, "even if she's always up to shenanigans. Takes after me!" Gramby June winked at that. "She'll be a late bloomer too. Why, I had the puniest aura in Nutfolk Wood until one day—*boom!* I was glowing like a sunrise. I tell you, that was the happiest day of my life. Yes, Winsome will be just like her old Gramby."

"What did you say her name was?" I asked, trying to recall when I'd heard it before.

"Winsome," Gramby answered. "Winsome Fall Nutbone—the little scamp."

Gramby June kept chatting easily but I could tell she was keeping an eye on Gramby Rain to check the progress of my arm. My brain was working sluggishly on identifying where I'd heard *Winsome*. And then I remembered. The voice in my tornado dream. "Win some, lose some." Her name was *Winsome*! She'd been making a joke. Had she *caught me in a dream* way back in the city? The doll on the post, beckoning to *turn here*. Winsome again?

"Did you *lead* me here to Wicket's Road?" I blurted.

"You led yourself, dear," Gramby Rain said gently. "You are stronger than you know. We just gave you a bit of . . . encouragement. Now turn your elbow just a fraction—that's right."

There was so much I wanted to know, I couldn't think clearly. This could be my only chance to talk to them, or this could all be dream and hallucination, with me breathing my last breath in the dirt. Whatever it was, I meant to make the best of it.

"Were you listening to Hazel, that day in the glen? I thought I saw you then."

"Well, we can't resist a good story, and that was right out of Rain's romantic years." Gramby Rain and Gramby June both chuckled at this.

"Why couldn't you let Hazel see you and still be her friend?" I asked, wanting to clear up this most basic mystery.

"All these years I was Hazel's friend," Gramby June said sincerely. "I'd catch her in dreams. I'd watch her from afar. She just lost sight of me because of the usual human trouble and worry. She couldn't help it. But I cherished that summer, and her friendship, and her simple words of wisdom. Hazel Wicket will always be my friend."

"Then why didn't you zap the bulldozer, and

the dirt bike? Why didn't you protect Hazel's land and your home?"

"It's the pesky engines, dear. Something about the electronics interferes with our senzall. That's why we sent the bees. We'd just then alerted a swarm when you stepped before the bike. But we all thank you for your gallant effort. We've made you an Honorable Citizen of Nutfolk Wood because on this day you were courageous, and so righteous in your courage."

The crowd spoke in unison, "Thank you, Willa Jane." Their little fingers pointed to their hearts and they bowed their heads down in the formal response. I was sure I recognized the crew supervisor, and the man named Stead.

"But those stupid Meeker guys—they tore up the glen. It looks awful," I moaned, feeling a lump of sorrow well up in my throat.

Gramby June dismissed this. "Oh pish-posh. We don't have Plum and her talents with us, but we do have some fine Plant Encouragers. We'll get things stumpshape in no time. Don't you worry about a thing."

"Did I see a crew of Encouragers the night of the full moon?"

"Well, no one mentioned a girl in the garden to *me*," she said with slight annoyance. "Only some silly gopher chase. But the farming senzall would have been thick. If you were there you'd have slept like a baby."

"I did. I slept hard. Gramby June—will I be able to see you when I wake up?" I asked hopefully.

"Maybe someday, dear. Maybe someday when you are pleased with this lovely earth, and pleased with your own lovely self. These are difficult times to be human. Things are so hurried and complicated. But you sought a peaceful place. And here you are."

My eyes opened warily. I braced for the pain that surely would come. But there was no pain. There was no dirt bike. And there were no Nutfolk.

I struggled to put the incidents into order. I was rammed by the bike, my arm smashed into the tree, and I dreamed—or saw—the little people of Nutfolk Wood!

Gramby Rain had said it was a nasty break. I fingered my arm gingerly, and though my sleeve was soaked in blood, there was no wound. I sat up, expecting some dizziness at least, but I felt okay. In fact, I felt really good.

A misty rain bathed my face. The quiet after the dirt bike was like velvet. The ground where the Nutfolk had stood was covered with the fragile violets. The world felt beautiful.

I was not afraid.

Heavy, clomping boots were jogging toward me. I turned to see a grim-faced Ed Meeker sprinting down the dozer trail. He was still speckled with the remains of all those bee stings.

"Jee-zus! My kid thought he'd killed you!" Ed boomed. "Danged idiot. What the heck did he think he was doing?" Ed complained about his son's trespassing and reckless driving, despite the fact that it was he, Ed, who had started all this nonsense the same way.

"Lemme take a look at that arm," Ed commanded. He seemed sober and genuinely concerned. Pulling up my sleeve, he gently twisted and poked. "Where'd all this blood come from?" he asked.

"I don't know. I must have scraped myself somewheres. It's all sort of a blur," I answered truthfully.

"Well, you can bet you'll get an apology from my son—dang moron. And I'd like to give you an apology myself, for driving down here drunk the other day. I shouldn't have done it, and I'm sorry you seen it." Ed Meeker's face flushed with the embarrassment of a man who rarely said he was sorry. I couldn't let him off the hook yet.

"I accept your apology," I said gravely. "But, Mr. Meeker, Hazel got sick over that whole deal. She went to bed that day, and hasn't been up since."

Ed let out a big sigh and shook his head. I could tell he was a man chock-full of trouble and worry. Finally Ed said, "Guess I need to square things with Miz Wicket. Can you walk?"

CHAPTER 21

An Oddball Gathering

I KEPT TELLING MR. MEEKER that I felt fine, but
he insisted on holding my arm in case I felt
faint.

We were approaching the Twig Bridge when we
saw Hazel shuffling toward us with unaccus-
tomed speed. She had thrown an afghan over her
nightie and slipped into her garden boots. Her
walking stick thumped forward with determina-
tion. She looked comical and pitiful at the same
time.

The moment she saw us her frantic expression
melted into relief, then hardened into fury.
"Edward Meeker, if you have harmed this child

I'll—I'll—" Hazel couldn't think of anything bad enough to do to Ed.

"I'm okay, Hazel. Really," I tried to assure her.

Mr. Meeker walked on with us to Hazel's house, explaining to Hazel about Michael and the dirt bike. He vowed that he would drag Michael's "sorry be-hind" over to make amends. We reached Hazel's, and surprisingly Ed asked if he could come in for a moment.

It was an odd-looking party of three: Hazel in her boots and afghan, Mr. Meeker with his bee-stung face, and me, splattered with dirt from head to toe. Hazel said she would put on some water for tea.

"Miz Wicket, I need to apologize for acting like a lunatic the other day," Ed Meeker announced humbly. "I don't recall what all I said, but I'm sure it was a bunch of hooey. I'd been tanked up for days. 'Course that's no excuse—makes it worse, in fact."

Ed sat uncomfortably at the table, looking

intently down at his hands clenched in his lap.

"That business in the woods—well, I couldn't go no lower," Ed said miserably. "I've been sober all this week," he added, like it was penance.

Hazel poured the boiling water into the teapot, and as she clinked and stirred she said, "I know it's been tough. I miss Rachel too."

I feared the big man would start to cry right there at the table. His eyes watered up, but he gained control and sighed a windy sigh.

"Ed," Hazel continued, "you got a couple of boys who need you. You got to pull out of this." Hazel moved over by Ed and laid a hand on his shoulder.

"I couldn't get no lower," Ed said again. Then he straightened his shoulders and looked Hazel in the eye. "So I'm headin' up."

Hazel seemed to understand what he was getting at, and gave him an approving nod. That's when we heard a timid knock at the screen door.

Michael and Vincent stood on the porch, looking

about as wretched and gawky as boys can look. Michael actually had his hat in his hands: an oily baseball cap that he'd crumpled into a wad. I could tell he'd been crying because his face and eyes were splotchy and red.

Right off, Michael said, "I didn't cut out 'cause I was scared. I figured you needed help, or an aid car or something. I'm—I'm sorry I was such a jerk."

"Well, I guess I'm okay," I said, feeling awkward over all the attention.

Michael looked doubtfully at my bloody sleeve. "You don't look okay," he said bluntly.

I smiled a little. "I generally don't look very good. But my arm is all right. I just need to find the scrape that made all this blood."

I noticed that Vincent's face was tense; his fists were balled up at his sides like he was ready for a fight. When I said I was okay, he visibly relaxed.

Mr. Meeker cleared his throat again and said, "Guess Mike and I will be over to mend the fence and smooth out the damage done, Miz Wicket. And I know Mike would want to pay for a new shirt for this girl." Ed cocked his head my way to indicate that I was "this girl." Michael nodded in obedient agreement.

Gruffly Ed added, "And, Vincent, I'm glad you dragged your brother over here. It was the right thing, son."

Vincent nodded stiffly at his father, and flushed at the rare compliment.

Then a car skidded to a halt out front, and Mama came bounding up the porch steps. "Where is she?" Mama demanded. Vincent had called her at the bookstore when Michael had come home blubbering about the girl he'd run over. Mama had driven about a hundred miles an hour to get here.

"Over here, Mama. And I'm fine."

"You don't look fine," challenged Mama, her eyes bugging out as she spied the bloody sleeve. She steered me into the bathroom and had me take off my shirt so she could find the mortal gash.

There was no gash. I couldn't explain it. Mama kept saying that I must have "nicked a pimple." The logic of this seemed to satisfy her. We borrowed a blouse from Hazel and returned to the oddball gathering.

Hazel was saying, "Ed, I appreciate the fence mending, but just leave well enough alone. I don't care for machinery in that glen. It compacts the soil."

Hazel wavered a little and closed her eyes. "I think I'd better put my feet up," she said in a creaky voice. "All this excitement has me feeling a might wobbly."

Hazel had been living on tea and toast for the last few days, and she had practically run up that trail—well, shuffled very quickly, anyway. She was probably ready to keel over.

"Here, Hazel, why don't you lie down for a bit?" I guided her over to the front-room sofa.

The gang followed us in, and as I got Hazel settled I noticed that Mr. Meeker was staring at the painting above the desk. He leaned in close to examine his wife's artwork. "*Nature's Magic*," he mumbled.

He startled us all by loudly blurting, "I just remembered something! Something Rachel asked me to tell you that last day in the hospital. She said, 'Tell Hazel to look behind nature's magic.' She didn't explain what she meant—just said to tell you. I should-a told you sooner, but with the funeral, and the booze—I guess I forgot," Ed said sheepishly.

"Look behind nature's magic? Does she mean there's something behind that old stump?" Hazel wondered from the couch, staring at the painting.

"Willa already had that idea," Vincent interjected. "We went down to the glen and dug all around that stump and didn't find squat."

"Maybe Rachel meant it philosophically," Hazel said, "like we ought to remember to enjoy these woods."

"Hazel," I said with my neck tingling, "maybe the title wasn't a description. Maybe Rachel left you *instructions*. I think we ought to look behind the darn picture!"

I removed the painting from its hook, and set it facedown on the coffee table. The back was neatly finished with brown paper, glued from edge to edge. Poking my finger through the taut paper, I ripped a big triangle out, revealing a layer of cardboard tacked into place.

"I need some pliers," I ordered like a surgeon.

"In the junk drawer," Hazel said.

Vincent ran to fish out the pliers and returned. I removed the slender tacks one by one. Finally I gripped a corner of the cardboard and pulled it out. The frame was a hefty one, deep-set and old-fashioned. There was a lot of room in that frame— room for a lot of pictures. Everyone gasped.

CHAPTER 22

A Fine Summer

O NE BY ONE, I removed Rachel's sketches rendered on stiff, heavy paper: gorgeous watercolors of Hazel's house, the glen, the stump, and the fairies of Nutfolk Wood.

Many of the paintings depicted the daily life of the little people dressed in their brown and green work clothes. There were children at Learning Circle, mothers hanging laundry, and fathers carrying babies. There were sailboats on the pond, parties on the shore, and cabins in a cluster. There was even a nighttime scene with men carrying globes on fishing poles, the spitting image of my dream!

And there was the Nutbone stump, trimmed out in green shutters, clever balconies, and the arch-topped door with the family crest.

Another study showed the crest up close—the crossed bones and the acorns and a curlicued inscription, which read: PEACE AND COURAGE, NUT-BONE.

Peace and courage! The words that led me *here*. Winsome had uttered them in my dream and they'd appeared on the Wicket's Road sign when I felt sick. "Turn here!" I had commanded.

Here was my evidence. Here was Hazel's Nutfolk summer, like a dream come true.

"Oh my!" Hazel exclaimed. "Oh my land!" she said for want of words. She began to softly weep.

I lifted out the last painting, and a note fluttered out and fell to the floor. It read:

> *Dear Hazel,*
> *I hope you will accept these paintings*

as a gift. I hesitated giving them out-
right because I wasn't sure it was the
proper thing. But I guessed if you were
searching for answers, you might look
here.

Don't be sad for me. I had some
good luck and magic, and lived longer
than my doctors ever thought possi-
ble. My last summer was my finest.
We'll always have nature's magic,

Your soul sister,
Rachel Meeker

It was an unlikely and lovely afternoon.
Everyone drank tea, and chitchatted, and
laughed a lot. We all seemed to feel good and
positive—like we'd each seen our troubles for
what they were, and making them right didn't
seem so hard anymore.

By afternoon the crowd had filtered out, leaving just Hazel and me. The house was quiet.

Ol' Cougar came out of hiding and jumped onto Hazel's lap. He'd been steering clear of her since she'd been "feeling poorly."

Hazel looked peaceful and happy. She was tired but in good spirits. I told her I'd fix her a can of soup. She said that would be "just the ticket."

"What do you think about all this?" I asked as I set down the soup and crackers.

"I think it helps me."

"Gives you some proof you mean?"

"Truth to tell," Hazel said thoughtfully, "we don't know whether Rachel *saw* the Nutfolk or whether she drew my descriptions. And that note is just vague enough to keep us guessing."

My spirits plummeted. Hazel was absolutely right.

"But that leaves us with a big, fat question mark! We still don't have proof positive!" I moaned.

"We may not have 'proof positive,' but I've made up my mind. Maybe I am an old kook, but I believe I saw something that summer. I saw something because I was special."

Making up her mind made Hazel look stronger and rejuvenated.

"Now I just need to get back on my feet and quit acting 'old and sick and lying around like a blob.'" Hazel quoted me with a suppressed smile on her face.

"I'm sorry I yelled at you," I said meekly.

"Well I'm not sorry. It was just what the doctor ordered. Got me out of my pity party." Quietly she added, "As long as I'm kicking, you can count on me, Miss Wil."

"Oh, Hazel!" I threw my arms around her and a sob escaped me because I was so relieved. Yet part of me was mournful, too. I knew she wouldn't live forever. I realized that sometimes all you get is bits—bits of time, or beauty, or friendship. My bit of friendship with Hazel was limited, but it was worth whatever it would cost.

Hazel hugged me and patted my back the way she'd patted Mama.

"Besides," she said kindly, "us soul sisters have to stick together."

I bobbed my head yes. I couldn't speak with a throat full of tears. I meant to tell her that she could count on me, too.

I took a step back from Hazel and squeegeed off some tears with my hand. "Hazel, did you tell Rachel about the family crest—about it saying 'peace and courage'?"

"Yes, I told her, Miss Detective."

"Just checking. I only wish I could have found proof positive—you know, hard evidence that it wasn't all in my head. I thought we had it. I was so sure."

"Could be there is no evidence," Hazel said wistfully. "Could be we've got bats in our belfry." She made a goofy face. "Guess it's just a matter of what you believe. Anyway, the journey was fun, wasn't it? I mean, it was a fine summer, no matter how you look at it."

"It was a fine summer, Hazel. It was the best."

CHAPTER 23

I Would Like to Believe

"**H**AVE YOU SEEN IT? It grew back in a week!"
I announced triumphantly.

"I saw it," Vincent admitted.

"There's no tire tracks," I said excitedly, "and no bulldozer road. It's like none of it ever happened."

The glen was green again, thick with new weeds and violets. I hiked out there every day to watch the progress. Vincent remained neutral on the subject, but I was thrilled.

"Quit wiggling!" Vincent ordered. He sat on a lawn chair in the middle of our driveway, a wide clipboard in his lap, and his paints at his side. The

gingersnaps were handy at his feet. He was painting me.

I sat on the front porch of the Gypsy Wagon
surrounded by some spindly roses that Hazel had
helped Mama transplant. I hoped they would
take, and Mama would have her little "house"
with the roses.

I was barefoot in overalls and a red shirt. I held
a fat bouquet of blue hydrangeas, which were the
best flowers we could find on this last day of
August.

"I feel like a goof," I said. "I hope no one drives
up—they'll think you're painting a scarecrow."

"You should quit putting yourself down,"
Vincent counseled. "You don't look nearly as
sickly as when you first got here. In fact, in certain lights you look almost not ugly." He smirked
over his well-delivered insult.

"Thanks a lot. With friends like you, who needs
enemies?"

Vincent smiled but did not retaliate. He

was busy painting.

"Mama said she might have to hire someone else for the bookstore. She said business is hopping. Plus Vivian wants to sell coffee, too, and make it like a reading café. Isn't that a cool idea?"

Vincent grunted.

"Guess what?" I asked, not waiting for an answer. "My uncle Andrew went on a date with Vivian! She said he looks like Grizzly Adams, but he's as 'sweet as sugar.'" I smirked thinking about it.

Vincent rolled his eyes and would not condescend to romantic gossip.

"I met the principal at Cedar Road," I chattered on. "Mama and I looked around the school, and the principal said I could enter either as a fourth grader or a fifth grader. He'd been looking at my work from last year, so he said if I want an easy year I could redo the fourth, or if I want to work hard I could manage the fifth."

"What are you gonna do?" Vincent asked.

"What do you think I should do?" I asked back.

"Well, if *you* want to sit with me on the bus, you gotta be a fifth grader because a sixth grader can't sit with a punky fourth grader."

"Okay."

"Okay what?"

"Okay I'll go in as a fifth grader. But you gotta promise to sit with me because I'm scared of the bus."

"Oh, the big yellow bus is so scary!" Vincent replied in falsetto.

I had to laugh. "It's not the bus, it's the kids."

"Oh, the little children are so scary!" he warbled again.

I laughed out loud and got scolded for moving.

"I mean I'm scared of being *the new kid*, Mr. Dense." I smiled to myself at the exchange. Vincent had a way of evaporating my fears. He had been different lately—happier, funnier. He didn't walk around with that chip on his shoulder all the time. Since his father had quit drinking, life at the Meeker house had settled into something more solid and sane. It was good for Vincent, I could tell.

I thought of my own father. "My dad is coming up for my birthday—I can't wait!"

I pictured Daddy all tan and handsome and full of praise for the Gypsy Wagon. He'd flip me upside down, and pick me up by my feet and say, "Gee, honey, you sure look different." Then of course *I* would say, "Those are my feet!" He'd set me upright and hug me tight—even though I don't like getting squeezed—but it would be okay. It would all be okay.

"Mama said I shouldn't get any ideas about her and Daddy getting back together. I told her it *did* cross my mind. She said to *forget it*. Oh well."

"You're doin' all right," Vincent said simply. "And so is your mom."

"I guess."

My thoughts bounced back to the birthday party, and I snickered a little, recalling the phone call to Grandma.

"We invited my Grandma Cookie to my birthday. Mama told her right off on the phone that she wasn't allowed to say anything critical. Well, Grandma couldn't keep still for even *one* minute, so she got herself *un*invited real fast."

I felt a certain devilish pleasure over Mama being so firm with Grandma Cookie. Mama said it was high time she stand up to her mother, and hoped eventually that Grandma would get a clue.

"Oh yeah, and you're invited, and so is Hazel," I finished brightly.

"Do I have to bring you a present?" Vincent asked, straight-faced.

"It is customary, ya cheapskate."

"Well, I guess I could spare a buck," Vincent conceded.

"Ha," was my brilliant response. "Are you almost done?" I asked, fidgeting.

"Quit wiggling! Jeez—now the angle's all wrong." Vincent strode to the porch with a long-suffering expression. He tilted my face and repositioned my arm. "There. Now don't move."

He resumed painting and I concentrated on being still. Finally he cleaned his brush and said, "Done."

I scrambled around behind him, eager to see the finished product.

"But this girl is pretty!" I blustered. She had shoulder-length brown hair that glinted auburn in the sun. Her face was thin but her smile was wide. Her eyes were deep brown and twinkling. She had a mischievous look about her. "Why'd you make me look so . . . cute?"

Vincent was growing annoyed. "Are you telling me I can't paint?"

"'Course you can paint!" I was hugely impressed. "It's a beautiful painting. You really are good, Vincent."

Vincent's face and ears glowed red. "Well, it's yours if you want it. Happy Birthday."

My first impulse was to hug him, but I knew

that would just embarrass him more, so I punched him hard on the shoulder. "Yeah, I want it!"

My bliss over the flattering painting was interrupted when Vincent muttered, "That's weird."

"What's weird?" I was compelled to ask.

"This thing on your arm." He licked his finger and scratched at my elbow. "Did you draw this on yourself, Wil?"

"What are you talking about?"

"Is this a birthmark?" Vincent persisted.

I twisted my arm backward, exasperated. I was sure that Vincent was teasing me. Then I saw it, plain as day. The perfect, dainty shape of an acorn.

Like a delicate tattoo, the acorn had appeared on the spot where Gramby Rain had placed her healing touch. The hair on the back of my neck rose.

"Maybe they really are out there," I whispered. "Maybe there is such a thing!"

"Are you talking fairies again?" Vincent asked, grave with doubt.

"When I was knocked out, and I had that dream—well, that's the spot where the healer said I had a nasty break. Right there is where she touched me! And she said, 'We've made you an honorable citizen of Nutfolk Wood.' This is so weird."

Mama called, "Supper's on! Vincent, you want to stay?"

As usual, Vincent responded, "Yeah, I'm hungry."

"Of course," I muttered. "Listen, Vincent—what do you think about all this? I mean, what do you really think about Hazel and the Nutfolk?"

"I really like Hazel," Vincent answered carefully, "but I think her stories got out of hand is all."

"So you think she just imagined everything?"

"She is pretty old, Wil."

"And do you think *I* imagined the things I saw?"

"You *were* sorta sickly for a while," Vincent answered with his brand of subtlety.

"But what about this—what about the acorn?" I challenged, thrusting my arm in his face.

Vincent examined it again. "It could be a freckle you never noticed. Or maybe it's a messed-up mole." He was determined to be skeptical.

I rolled my eyes. "Well, I would like to *believe*," I said finally. "And I almost do, except I don't want to be disappointed."

"Don't let that stop you." Vincent grinned. "I thought you were trying to not be such a weenie."

"You be quiet!" I commanded, and I tried to whack him but he dodged me too quickly.

I felt a wave of joy, full to the brim with happiness. "Maybe there *are* fairies in this forest," I said in my most mysterious voice. "*And maybe I'm just the girl to find them.*"

Vincent looked at me straight on, and smiled appraisingly. "Maybe you are," he agreed.

"Go wash up," Mama ordered from the porch.

The sun was melting to amber, hinting at the day's end. Mama had been right about storms not lasting forever. My sun had come out by and by.

For a little longer Vincent and I stood in the driveway gazing at the country girl in the painting. She was rosy-cheeked and grinning, and looked like a girl I knew.

Epilogue

Dear Daddy,

How are you? I am fine. Sorry I didn't write more, but I wasn't sure what to say.

I learned a lot this summer. Not so much about school stuff, but about fixing up the trailer, and planting plants, and making new friends. And I learned about a certain girl who was very upset about a certain divorce. Guess who?

I was sort of mad that you left. Everything seemed so different and I *couldn't do anything about it. But by the time summer was over, I didn't feel so rotten since I think I ended up in just the right place. Here on Wicket's Road.*

When you visit, I want to tell you the story of my summer and how it all happened. It's a good story, about Hazel and me, and fairies that live in the woods.

And don't worry, it ends happily ever after.

I miss you,
Love, Willa

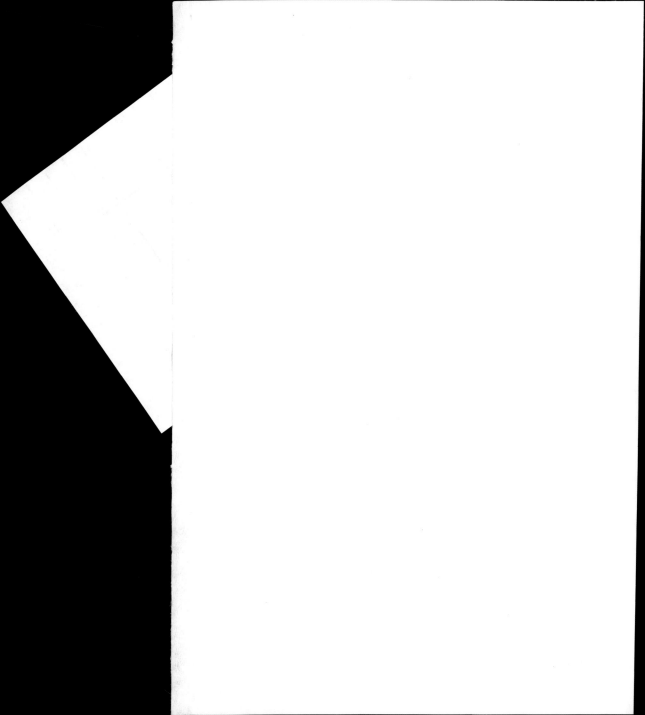

Rosa Parks Elementary School
22845 NE Cedar Park Crescent
Redmond, WA 98053